ALL THE
STARS
LOOK DOWN

All The Stars Look Down

A Duo of Christmas Romances

Grace Draven
and
Elizabeth Hunter

ALL THE STARS LOOK DOWN

Sunday's Child
Copyright © 2014
Grace Draven

Lost Letters and Christmas Lights
Copyright © 2014
Elizabeth Hunter

ISBN 13: 9781505438895
ISBN 10: 1505438896

SUNDAY'S CHILD

Grace Draven

*SUNDAY'S CHILD is dedicated to my
two favorite guys:
my husband Patrick and my son Brendan –
that beloved puzzle piece.*

PROLOGUE

Were it something more meaningful or noble, Andor Hjalmarson wouldn't think twice about choosing execution over such humiliation, but to willingly die because he coaxed the wrong woman to his bed made him one idiotic martyr. He was neither an idiot nor a martyr.

His aunt, the Supremely Divine, Majestically Beautiful, and Eternally Sublime Dagrun of Ljósálfheimr pinned him with a glare colder than sharpened icicles. "You are an idiot," she declared.

Andor stiffened but held his tongue. He balanced on the thin edge of Dagrun's mercurial mercy. A glib remark, or even a rebellious one, and she might well rescind her offer that allowed him to keep his head attached to his shoulders.

The sainted, immortal Nicholas of Myra stood beside him, not at all pleased to find himself dragged into such an awkward situation but still willing to help the ljósálfar queen's troublesome nephew. "I can keep him busy for the length of his exile, but his skills will be wasted with me. You'll lose a capable warrior, Your Majesty."

"And you'll gain one, Nicholas." A black scowl marred Dagrun's perfect features. "And keeping him busy is exactly what he needs. He obviously has too much time on his hands if he's running about Ljósálfheimr seducing all of Algr's concubines."

"I seduced one," Andor protested. "The least of the king's favorites."

"Silence." Dagrun rose from her throne. Her graceful strides carried her across the length of the throne room until she stood within inches of Andor. He lowered his eyes before her glacial stare. "The only reason your head isn't mounted on the gates of Niflheimr is because of Algr's affections for me and his recognition of my affections for you—which are fast souring."

The queen swept back to her chair, her gown's long train shimmering with the ethereal light cast by far off Asbrú. Andor's eyebrows rose as Dagrun's gaze found the venerable saint once more, and her features softened. Had there once been more than friendship between the ljósálfar queen and this Christian bishop made immortal?

"I place Andor in your capable hands, Nicholas. Surely, a thousand years under your tutelage will teach him respect and caution."

Andor almost blurted out such exile would likely only teach him boredom. He kept the words behind his teeth as Dagrun's eyes narrowed.

Nicholas tucked his vestments around him and smoothed his beard. He bowed to the queen. "I will do my best, Your Majesty." He glanced at Andor, the expression in his eyes both resigned and wary. "Ready, son?"

Before Andor could answer or protest, the saint tapped the end of his crosier twice on the marble floor, and the realm of Ljósálfheimr disappeared. His exile had begun.

CHAPTER ONE

N icholas wondered if he'd fallen from favor with the elf queen. What other explanation could there be for her sending him the most prideful, stubborn creature to walk any plane of existence? If he wasn't already a saint, dealing with Andor Hjalmarson for a thousand years–and a day–without killing him would guarantee Nicholas canonization. As it was, he braced himself for another of the countless arguments he'd had with the elf over the centuries.

Andor scowled, arms crossed. "Every house celebrating Christmas in Philadelphia now has a few unique gifts under the tree, as you requested."

Nicholas rubbed his temples. Andor's interpretation of help during Christmas delivery often involved unexpected chaos. "Would you care to explain your actions at the Wilmington household?"

"Not really."

"Andor, you stripped a man down to his underwear, tied him to the banister with tree garland–which I'm certain you strengthened–and set off the house alarm on purpose!"

"What was I supposed to do? He was robbing them! Don't you think there's something a little pointless to delivering gifts to people just so others can steal them?"

The saint began to pace, his long bishop's robes filthy from a long night of world travel. His back hurt; he was hungry, bone-weary, and desperately needed sleep. Having a small crowd of his gnomes meet him at the gates when he returned with yet another tale of Andor's escapades wasn't exactly how he wanted to end the Season.

"If you felt the need to interfere, you could have done so in a less obvious manner."

Andor refused to budge in his defense. "I left him without a single bruise." He smiled. "Though he cried as if I'd broken every bone in his body."

Nicholas groaned. "Son, I can see why your people thought you strange. You have a sense of justice and compassion they don't possess, and it's been honed over the years. But you have a clumsy way of going about it. I have a reputation to uphold— kindly, giving, jolly and all that. Children won't want to stay up and catch a glimpse of me if it becomes known Santa travels with a vigilante elf."

Andor's hands curled into fists. Like Nicholas, he began to pace, his long legs eating up the space in the cozy parlor.

"Why not a vigilante? A protector? Have you kept track of how many times we've been shot at, fired upon and attacked over the years? I took a crossbow bolt in the leg from John Peasant in 1343 while leaving a gift at the end of his child's bed. Remember that?"

"He mistook you for a leprechaun bent on mischief."

Andor growled low in his throat. "Shows what good it does me to glamour myself as one of your nisse so I don't scare people."

He had a point. Despite the frivolity and light-heartedness associated with Saint Nicholas and the Christmas season, it was a dangerous business. Nicholas himself carried a few souvenir scars from Christmases past.

He was saved from arguing further by a polite knock on his door. "Enter."

The door opened, admitting Carolan, one of the diminutive nisse chiefs. His ears, pointed like Andor's, but much longer and more pronounced, twitched in agitation. "Forgive me, Nikolai, but we have a problem."

Nicholas stopped short of another groan. There was a hot pot of tea waiting for him and a comfortable bed ready for when he finally had a chance to sleep. It looked as if he might not see either for some time to come. "What now, Carolan?"

"You bypassed a delivery."

"What?!"

The gnome pulled a small scroll out of his pocket. "Indeed. One Claire Summerlad, age seven, Dallas, Texas."

Andor snorted. "Not my fault. You assigned me the east."

The saint passed a hand over his eyes. "I'm getting too old for this."

"You've been the same age for almost seventeen hundred years. That's not much of an excuse."

Nicholas laughed, the sound booming off the walls. Andor had gotten in a small dig, one that restored Nicholas's good humor, despite his weariness. "Touché, Andor." He nodded to Carolan. "I'll take care of it now. It's one household, a meager one at that. There won't be much to bring."

The nisse chief bowed. "I'll have her things waiting when you're ready."

After he left, Nicholas turned to Andor. "You're welcome to join me."

Andor raised an eyebrow. "You trust I won't do something against your rules?"

Nicholas chuckled. Despite his many transgressions during his long servitude to the saint, Andor remained one of his favorite helpers. The nisse didn't always understand his tolerance for the unruly, often haughty elf, but they hadn't witnessed what Nicholas had.

The early years of the twentieth century had been bleak ones, when men seemed hell-bent on destroying each other in the travesty known as the Great War. Millions died on hillsides and in trenches from wounds and disease. The greatest drain on his magic had taken place then, when gifts weren't toys or trinkets but nearly dead hope, a pail of food to eat, a loved one returned alive from the battlefield.

It was during one of those years they had passed over a field carved into a maze of trenches. The December air was icy, filled with the scent of sulfur. Nicholas had sent Andor to a small village nearly razed to the ground by war. Only two families remained, widows with children and an old man. When he returned for the elf, he wasn't at their appointed meeting place. Instead, Nicholas found him in one of the trenches.

A soldier, gut-shot and bleeding out, lay dying in the frozen mud. He was no more than eighteen, and Nicholas remembered him as a small child, vibrant and determined to catch Pére Noël stuffing his shoes with treats by the fireplace.

Andor crouched over him, his graceful hands bloodied as he spread them over the boy's wound. Nicholas remained silent as the elf spoke softly, ancient words of ljósálfar power that brought comfort and a surcease of pain.

The boy's stark face relaxed, turned peaceful as he stared up at Andor. "Are you an angel?"

Andor's pale, unearthly beauty took on an ethereal glow, magic pouring from him as he met the soldier's gaze.

"If that's what you wish."

"I don't want to die alone."

Andor's voice chimed like the music of bells. "You're not alone. Your forefathers await you."

The boy's expression turned beatific as he looked past Andor's shoulder to a spot beyond the world's reality. "It's Christmas," he said.

"Yes."

"Merci," he said on a gentle sigh. His eyes glazed over, and he was gone.

Andor passed a hand over the soldier's face to close his eyes. "You're welcome."

When he climbed out of the trench, his broad shoulders were bowed. He looked to Nicholas. "There's much death here."

Nicholas clapped a hand on Andor's shoulder. "Come, lad. We've more to do this night."

That moment had forever changed the saint's view of Andor Hjalmarson, and while his antics during the Season sometimes drove Nicholas to distraction, he'd never forgotten the elf's compassion.

"Nicholas?" Andor's question, laced with impatience, brought him out of his reverie.

"Hmmm?"

"Are you certain you trust me enough to behave?"

"No, but I want you along anyway. Gather your things. We've a small girl to visit."

Chapter Two

The home Nicholas had accidentally bypassed in his deliveries was on the second floor of a derelict apartment building that looked as if it wouldn't pass the laxest building code. The foundation sank at one corner, causing large cracks to stairstep up the brick walls. Balcony railings hung loose from their moorings or were missing altogether. Windows were cracked or completely shattered, trash littered the walkways, and in one very dark corner of the building a man tightened a makeshift tourniquet around his arm and reverently kissed the plastic chalice of a hypodermic needle.

Andor followed Nicholas up the stairs to Claire Summerlad's apartment. In his centuries among them, the elf had seen the rise and fall of men and their civilizations. He'd been amused and admiring to watch great minds figure out the world was round, how gravity worked, what made the light bulb shine and how to fly to the moon. He'd been equally horrified to watch the white mushroom cloud explode skyward. Men had surpassed the álfar. They had become god-like in their ability to destroy.

Yet, for all their knowledge, their power and their creature comforts, they were sometimes reduced to this—running poison through their veins in a futile attempt to stave off an internal darkness.

"Leave him be, Andor. He's far beyond any small comfort we can give him."

Nicholas's voice brought him out of his reverie, and he was surprised to find himself back at the bottom step. "He can't see us, Nicholas. What harm would it do?"

"None, but what good would it do? There's someone waiting for us, one whose belief is so powerful, it gives her strength and hope. That poor soul gave those up long ago."

Andor sighed. Nicholas was right. There were some too far gone for even his brand of magic to touch and ease. He jogged up the stairs on silent feet and followed Nicholas through the closed apartment door.

It was dark inside save for the single strand of twinkling lights wrapped around a tabletop artificial Christmas tree that looked as if it had been rescued from a dumpster. One small gift, wrapped in red paper, lay under its lopsided branches.

A faded couch and a lawn chair were pushed against one wall. Two egg crates, stacked one atop the other, supported an old TV. Garland made of construction paper loops hung above the window looking out onto the main walkway, and a child's hand-drawn pictures of Santa and all his entourage were taped on the walls in various places. This was an impoverished household, but one where the spirit of the season was alive and well.

Nicholas motioned with his hand, and both he and Andor became visible once more. The elf raised an eyebrow. "You don't often do that. Are you hoping she sees you?" He didn't bother whispering. The magic suffusing the apartment kept their voices silent to all save each other.

The shuffle and crackle of Christmas paper was loud in the room as Nicholas dug in the small bag he brought. Three colorful boxes wrapped in gold and silver paper, with cascades of ribbons pouring down their sides, joined the lone present. They were accompanied by unwrapped gifts as well—a stack of books and a sketch pad with artist pencils.

The saint's eyes twinkled. "You might want to glamour yourself, lad. She's coming down the hall now."

Andor had only seconds to overlay a glamour, that of one of Nicholas's nisses. Even after all these years, it still unnerved him when those children lucky enough to "catch" Santa and his helper looked at his knees when they spoke to him in their high, breathless voices.

Claire Summerlad, age seven, was a skinny, graceless child made up of knobby knees and elbows. Her short, blonde hair stuck out at all angles, testament to the rigors of a restless sleeper. She approached the door slowly, as wary as any creature who senses a strangeness to its surroundings.

From his vantage point, Andor had a clear view of her face when she caught sight of Nicholas standing next to her decrepit little tree with its array of gifts beneath it. Gray eyes widened to the size of dinner plates, and her mouth formed a silent "O" of amazement.

"Hello, Claire. Merry Christmas."

It never failed to send a tingle down Andor's spine when a child uttered Nicholas's name with such wonder. He felt it again when Claire spoke.

"Santa?"

Nicholas laughed, a great rolling thunder of mirth that made his beard shake and might have awakened the entire apartment complex if the magic didn't work to keep it contained. He held out his arms.

The child ran to him, but skidded to a stop when she caught sight of Andor off to the side. It was his turn to gape. Claire wasn't looking at his knees. Instead, her head was tilted back, eyes looking far up to his much greater height so she could meet his gaze.

His indrawn breath echoed louder than Nicholas's laughter. A Sunday's Child. Claire was a Sunday's Child, and one with enough of the Sight to see beyond his glamour. She walked closer until she was directly in front of him. Andor paused for a second, then crouched until he was eye-level with the girl.

Nicholas stood forgotten as, for uncounted moments, elf and human child stared at each other, enraptured. "What do you see?" he asked her softly.

A small hand rose, fluttered across his face. "Forever. I see Forever." She smiled, revealing a missing front tooth.

How rare a thing to find a Sunday's Child in this age of disbelief. Hundreds of years earlier, ljósálfr like himself would have hunted her, made her a changeling to live among them and guard against her betraying their presence with her deep Sight. Now they would take her just to assure themselves they hadn't completely faded from the world.

"I like your ears," she said. "They're very pointy." Claire grinned but didn't try to touch him.

Andor returned her smile. "They're my best feature."

"Andor." The elf dragged his gaze from Claire to Nicholas. "We have to leave."

"Yes."

Claire grabbed Andor's hand, startling him with her sudden action. "Don't go," she pleaded. "You can eat breakfast with us. My mom is making pancakes, and you can help me open presents."

It was difficult to free his hand from hers. He'd very much like to stay, but Nicholas was right. Their time among this world was fleeting, limited to a single season and a single night. Claire was luckier than most in that she saw Nicholas in all his Christmas glory. She was more unique than most in that she saw Andor in his true form.

He bowed before her, a courtly gesture usually reserved for Dagrun. "I'm sorry, Claire. We have to leave."

His stomach knotted when her gray eyes glazed with tears, but she held them back with a loud sniff. "Okay," she said in a wobbly voice. Her smile returned full force when she turned to Nicholas. "Thank you, Santa."

"My pleasure, Claire." Nicholas's voice deepened, gained a rhythm that vibrated deep into Andor's bones and made him a touch drowsy. "Now, I want you to go back to bed. The presents will still be here, and there's a special one for your mother, too."

Andor's brows rose, as did the saint's, when Claire managed to successfully fight off the sleep spell long enough to address Andor once more.

"Come see me next year. I won't forget you. You won't forget me?"

The knot in his belly tightened. She would forget, or cease to believe. Time and age would see to it, even for a Sunday's Child. The human adult changed belief systems, relegated the wonders of childhood sorcery to memories. Such knowledge never bothered him before. It did now.

"No, Claire. I won't forget you."

She nodded slowly, her eyelids drifting to half-mast over her eyes as the spell took effect. "Okay." She yawned twice and tottered out of the room. Her sleepy voice drifted back to them from the hall. "Goodnight."

The silence in the small living room held nothing of magic in it. Nicholas sighed, and there was an odd sympathy in his dark gaze. "You're lucky. We rarely come across one like her these days."

Andor closed his eyes. "I know, and I'm not sure if I should celebrate or grieve."

Chapter Three

"I've escaped the stacks for today, and I'm going home." Claire peered around the carpet wall separating her cube from Dee's. "Do you need anything from me before I go?"

Dee Howard glanced up from her monitor for a moment and paused in scribbling notes in a ratty notebook. She blinked at Claire as if trying to remember who she was. "I'm sorry. What?"

Claire sighed. As one of the archivist employed by the Carmichael Research Institute and Museum, she worked closely with the curatorial staff on multiple projects. For the past three months, she'd been hip-deep with Dee in preparation for the illuminated manuscript exhibit Dee was coordinating. There were times she thought she'd have to bring up a blanket and pillow and sleep in the repositories room just to get half the work done for this project. She was suspicious Dee was already doing just that.

"I'm leaving for the night. You should too. It's after 6:00, and you've been here since at least 5:30 this morning."

A puzzled frown knitted Dee's brow. "How do you know that?"

"Time stamp on the first e-mail I got from you today." Claire shrugged on her coat. "Gotta go. Ian will be wondering where I am."

Dee's phone rang. She answered and held up a finger to Claire in a silent request to wait. Claire used the opportunity to fish her purse out of one of her desk drawers. By the time she'd dug her keys out of a side pocket, Dee had finished the call and left her cube.

"I'll walk with you," she offered. "That was Andor. The first crate from the Matenadaran just arrived at the loading dock." Her voice virtually quivered with excitement.

Claire made to tease Dee that she'd probably find her hugging the crate, waiting for the preparator crew to open it, but the odd, unfamiliar name sidetracked her. "Who's Andor?"

The staff at the Carmichael was relatively small compared to other larger museums like the Houston Museum of Fine Arts or Natural Science. Claire had worked at the Carmichael for four years; she knew most everyone, at least by name. She didn't recognize the name Andor.

Dee halted her with a hand on her elbow. She gaped at Claire. "You haven't met Andor the preparator?"

Claire burst out laughing. Dee's description, delivered in tones of disbelief and amazement, conjured images of a murderous cyborg with one glowing red eye and a mission to wipe out all of mankind; that, or his name flashing in great big, flashing billboard lights. "Not that I remember, and I think I would have based on your reaction."

Dee whistled. "Oh yeah, you would remember meeting him. Prime eye candy. Too bad he's only temp. On loan from the Menil to help out while Paul is on medical leave."

Their senior preparator had hurt his back during setup of a sculpture exhibit. For most of the year, the crew made do through any shortages of manpower, but during Christmas, the Carmichael was insanely busy, and the loss of even one person had an obvious ripple effect. Claire was surprised the Menil, far busier than the Carmichael, had been willing to loan out of its preparators even temporarily.

The two women passed through hallways of closed office doors and file rooms until they reached the loading docks. Two large trucks were parked in the bays, one with its trailer doors open and a parade of people carting out containers on dollies and pallet jacks.

Dee raised her hand and waved at someone in the crowd. "Andor!"

Claire looked to where Dee waved and spotted a tall man with a blond ponytail checking off something on a clipboard. He turned and waved at Dee.

"Wait until he gets closer," Dee said. "It's almost criminal that a man can be that good looking."

Claire gave her a dubious look. Were it anyone other than the reserved, serious Dee who made such a remark, she would have rolled her eyes. This guy must be something for her friend to wax so girlish over someone's looks. "Blonds aren't my type," she said.

"You'll be a convert after this."

Dee didn't exaggerate. As Andor narrowed the distance between them, Claire tried not to let her jaw bang on the floor. There were many types and interpretations of beauty; she saw all aspects of it in her job at the museum. That which was earthy and coarse could be as pleasing as that which was refined and classical. Ugly was beautiful to some and beautiful, flat and boring to others. It truly was all in the eye of the beholder. Sometimes though, universal appeal reigned, and in this man's face resided the manifestation of perfect geometry and aesthetic appeal. Had this Andor lived a few hundred years earlier, Da Vinci would have painted him.

Claire's objective admiration for him gave way to a strange unease when he stopped before them and shook Dee's hand. "Good evening, Delilah."

His voice, warm and faintly accented, triggered vague recollections for Claire. Or maybe dreams. She frowned, her mind reaching for will-o-the-wisp memories of a hazy figure bathed in shimmering light that asked her a question. *"What do you see?"*

"Hey, Andor. I don't think you've met Claire, one of our archivists. Claire, Andor Hjalmarson. Andor, Claire Summerlad."

Claire held out her hand, still distracted by the odd notion she'd once heard Hjalmarson's voice a long time ago. Her distraction evaporated, chased away by the pleasant tingle that raced up her arm when he clasped her fingers and gave them a squeeze.

She withdrew her hand from his. His fingertips lingered on her palm before he let her go. She cleared her throat. "It's nice to meet you, Mr. Hjalmarson. We can definitely use the help." She silently congratulated herself on the normal pitch of her voice.

"A pleasure, Claire, and please call me Andor." He smiled, and Claire swore she heard Dee sigh.

He had the bluest eyes. Not lapis or sapphire or cerulean. More like deep winter ocean with a starburst of yellow and amber surrounding his pupils. Dark brown eyebrows and eyelashes contrasted with his much lighter hair. She might have compared him to an angel, but there was an earthiness to him that ruined the ethereal.

Dee knocked her in the side with an elbow. "You're staring," she murmured. She offered Andor a bright smile and rubbed her palms together. "So where's this crate you called me about?"

A heat wave scaled up Claire's chest, over her neck and flooded into her cheeks. She was staring, and by Andor's knowing half-smile, it was as obvious as the blush threatening to set her face and scalp on fire. The smile she gave him felt thin and stiff. "It's nice meeting you. I'm sure we'll see each other again soon."

He nodded, his blue eyes flaring hot as a star. "I look forward to it."

Dee's faint gasp mirrored her wide-eyed expression. Claire pretended not to notice her friend's speculative look as she glanced back and forth between her and Andor. "I gotta go. I'm already twenty minutes late getting out of here. Elise is going to have my head on a plate. See you tomorrow."

She gave a casual wave and fled, Andor Hjalmarson's gaze heavy on her back. If anyone later asked, Claire would lie through her teeth and say her jog out of the loading docks was because she had to relieve her son's caregiver. Nothing more. Nothing less. And nothing at all to do with the striking preparator who mesmerized her with only a handshake and an evocative voice.

Houston's typical evening gridlock was in full swing by the time she got out on the road. After thirty minutes and an apology-laced phone call to the babysitter, she pulled into the driveway of her tiny rent house and burst through the door.

"I'm so sorry, Elise," she said for the twenty-seventh time since leaving the museum parking lot."

The babysitter gave her a casual wave. "No worries. Nothing planned for tonight, and I'm sick of studying." She placed a bowl of pasta with pesto in front of the small, dark-haired boy seated at the dinner table. "He finished shredding the chicken tenders I fixed him, so we're on to the pasta."

She glanced at Claire. "I'll stay until you can change, run to the bathroom; all that before I head out. Jake and I are going to work on table manners." She pulled up a chair next to Jake and coaxed him to take a plastic spoon from her. "Come on, little dude. You can't be eating with your fingers all the time."

Claire skirted around the table and dropped a kiss on the boy's head. "Sorry I'm late, kiddo. I'll be right back." He didn't look up from the computer tablet Claire had bought him a year earlier. His favorite children's video played in a loop, the same three minute scene playing over and over while he held his spoon in a half-hearted grip and tucked pasta into his mouth.

Claire tossed her purse on the couch and disappeared into her bedroom to change into her favorite evening wear—sweats and a T-shirt. She'd wash away her makeup later. Elise was already well past her usual time.

She didn't know what she would do without Elise. The college kid looked after her son for the few hours after his bus dropped him off and Claire got home from work. Tattooed, pierced and impressively tall in a pair of heeled combat boots, the girl possessed endless patience and a sixth sense for knowing how to deal with an autistic child. Claire considered her a blessing for Jake and herself.

After Elise left for the evening, Claire sat down next to Jake and finished off the remainder of the lukewarm pasta and pesto. Jake pushed his half-eaten portion aside and turned his full attention to his video. He made odd noises, some Claire could translate, others she couldn't; high-pitched yips combined with snatches of songs and the odd line or two from other movies. They almost never made sense in context, but the words he uttered were clear and well-articulated.

Claire tried to think of those noises as progress. Two years ago, Jake was completely silent. After their dinner, she tucked him into his favorite corner of the couch and sat next to him, sharing a blanket. Except for the TV's low volume and Jake's movie on his tablet, the house was quiet.

Most every evening was like this, even the weekend. Claire didn't mind the lack of a social life too much. She'd always been introverted. Even when she was in school, single and Jake not even a gleam in her eye, she'd found nothing appealing about hanging out in bars and pubs packed with people and virtually bulging the walls with a cacophony of too-loud music and couples shouting at each other to be heard over the din. Sometimes though, she missed a night out with friends.

Andor Hjalmarson's handsome features rose in her mind's eye. Claire didn't try to suppress the image. Dee was right. One brief meeting, and he'd made her a convert to liking blonds. He'd been a perfect gentleman during their introduction, but Claire still felt the residual tingle in her arm from when he'd shaken her hand and the heaviness of his gaze on her back when she'd left the loading dock. And she still couldn't shake the strange sense that he was somehow connected to the hazy childhood memory of shimmering light and a beguiling voice.

"What do you see?"

Jake suddenly leaned to the side and pressed his lips to her arm, startling Claire out of her reverie. She smiled, hugged him to her and kissed his forehead. "Thanks for the kiss, buddy. Time for a bath, and since Elise gave you pesto, I'll probably have to boil your teeth instead of just brushing them tonight." She patted him on the knee. "Come on. Let's go."

Once she had Jake in bed and his backpack ready for school the next day, Claire finished her own bedtime preparations. She slid under the covers, set her alarm and stared wide-eyed into the darkness. The holidays were bearing down her like a train. She and Jake didn't go anywhere or do much for either Thanksgiving or Christmas, but the museum was in high gear with two Christmas exhibits and the upcoming benefits dinner dance and charity auction. She had a lot of long hours ahead of her.

She smiled. At least she and Dee had something more to admire than miles of garland and forests of decorated Christmas trees. As Dee said, Andor was primo eye candy, and while Claire might be divorced, overworked, and socially clueless when it came to dating, she wasn't blind. She'd just have to be a little more circumspect in her admiration of the new preparator.

"I can do calm, cool and suave," she said aloud, trying to convince herself. She snorted. Yeah right. She turned on her side and closed her eyes, happy to fall asleep to the memory of deep-ocean eyes.

CHAPTER FOUR

The gangly Sunday's Child with straggly hair and a missing tooth was gone. Claire Summerlad had grown into a woman of elegance with fine, somber features and guarded eyes. Their very first meeting, when she'd seen through his glamour and entranced him with the discovery that Sunday's Children were still in the world, had also been the last between them.

Nicholas's magic was different from ljósálfr magic, bestowed by a divine force unrelated to the Ljósálfrheimr realm and resistant to Claire's deep Sight. The saint could visit the girl's house each year unseen if he wished. Andor couldn't, and Nicholas had been adamant that the elf avoid any children like Claire, no matter how rare, at all costs.

"This is a century that ridicules magic, Andor. Claire's Sight isn't a gift. Because she's a child, people will think her just highly imaginative and indulge her. As she grows older, that indulgence will become concern and suspicion. Claire herself will question the soundness of her mind if she sees and hears things no one else does. It's better that she let her Sight fade and her memory of you become the dream of a childhood she'll set aside."

For some odd reason, that last part had turned Andor's stomach, but he did as Nicholas counseled and never saw Claire again, until their meeting on the Carmichael's loading docks. She had stared at him with a weary gaze that no longer saw wonder or the ljósálfr elf whose pointed ears she once complimented. He hadn't missed the puzzled flicker of recognition in her eyes—as if the shadow of that distant Christmas Eve teased her memory—or her embarrassed blush at being caught staring at him with very womanly admiration.

Andor watched her surreptitiously this morning as he and another preparator opened boxes and filled out condition reports on one of the long tables in the conservation lab. Claire, Dee and one of the conservators unpacked boxes at another table. Their Nitrile-gloved hands looked like doves as they checked each illuminated manuscript sent from the Matenadaran for damage and cataloged their contents.

Despite time and her maturity, Andor recognized Claire instantly when they met two days earlier on the loading docks. Her Sight had faded just as Nicholas predicted, and she didn't see past the glamour that humanized his features and disguised the distinctive shape of his ears. He'd worn this particular spell so often and for so long while among humans that it rested as comfortably on him as an old shirt. Still, it wasn't enough to lessen his vague disappointment that while Claire might admire him, she didn't truly see him. He disagreed with Nicholas that her Sight had not been a gift.

"Uh oh." Dee frowned at the box in front of her.

The much taller Claire leaned over her shoulder. "Missing the bill of lading?"

"No, it's there. But just the Armenian version. Either the English translation got lost or someone forgot to put it on."

Claire shrugged. "E-mail the curator and ask for another copy. They're what, eight hours ahead of us? By the time you get in tomorrow, they'll have replied."

Andor approached their table. "I can read Armenian."

Three sets of gazes settled on him and stayed. Claire and the conservator each raised an eyebrow. Dee tilted her head to one side. "Well, aren't you just full of surprises?"

If she only knew. Andor smiled, not at all offended by their doubts. Houston was a huge metropolis with a diverse population that encompassed numerous linguistic families. English, Spanish, and Vietnamese were the most commonly spoken. Armenian was considerably more rare.

"I'm fluent in several languages." A thousand years of exile in Midgard had provided ample time to learn the many tongues of the humans.

Claire slid the list to him, her mouth tilted in a faint smile. "What does it say?"

He translated the bill, pausing only when Dee held up her hand. "We're convinced," she said.

"Read it again, and we'll report and catalog as you go."

An hour later, Andor left the lab for one of the exhibit halls where another team of preparators worked to set up an exhibit of 19th century art glass. The sound of footsteps paced on a long stride drifted to his ears. His heartbeat sped up. Claire.

"Mr. Hjalmarson, wait."

He stopped and turned. She offered him a wider, friendlier smile than the one she gave in the lab. It transformed her features in subtle ways. The hollows below her cheekbones filled out, and her eyes sparkled, reminiscent of the young girl who saw an elf for the first time, standing in her mother's living room. The refined angles of her face softened and warmed. Andor thought her lovelier than any ljósálfr woman.

"Just Andor is fine," he said. "The only people who address me by my last name are my accountant and the police."

Her eyebrows shot up and the smile wavered a little. "Do you often deal with the cops?"

He grinned. "Not in the way you're thinking." Her skin pinked at his teasing. "Two speeding tickets is the extent of my life of crime." At least by the definition of 21st century laws. He chose not to mention that caveat.

She chuckled. "Oh, well then, I'm a more hardened criminal than you. Two speeding tickets and an expired tag."

Curious as to why she sought him out, Andor didn't continue their banter. "What can I do for you, Ms. Summerlad?"

Her blush returned a little rosier this time. "Please call me Claire. I hope I didn't insult you with my doubt about your claim to read Armenian. It just seemed too convenient to be true. Our temp preparator helping us at just that moment and also fluent in a language not at all common in this city? No one gets that lucky, you know?"

Andor shrugged. "No offense taken. And maybe it was more fate than luck."

Claire laced her fingers together and clasped them in front of her. "Paul will be back and you at the Menil before Dee gets started on the main work of her exhibition. However, I've already begun work on research and provenance for some of the illuminated manuscripts we received from the Fitzwilliam and the Morgan. I've located texts that describe the manuscripts in more detail. Unfortunately, some of the descriptions aren't translated." She took a breath and continued. "I can hire out a translator, but having someone in-house who can do it would be a lot easier."

"You want me to translate for you?"

She nodded. "I do." Her hands came up in a gesture that warded off argument. "I know you're as busy as the rest of us with the Gallé exhibit and the upcoming benefits dinner, but if you can carve out any time to do a little translation, I'd be grateful. Weekends even if that's all you have. We'll expense it through my department, and I'll deal with accounting later."

Time with Claire, grown to adulthood and no longer aware of magic. This was definitely fate more than luck. Andor had a wary respect for the Norns and sensed Ver andi's weave in this scenario. If the jötunn giantess were here now, he'd thank her.

"Have lunch with me today," he said.

She backed up a step, and her arms crossed. Her eyes narrowed. "You'll help me with translations if I have lunch with you?" A touch of frost glazed her voice.

Since his exile, Andor had lived amongst humans, immersed in their ways and behaviors. Nicholas only required his presence a few days out of each year, and he'd embraced the saint's suggestion that he learn more of Midgard and its people, disguised as a human himself. Nicholas didn't voice what they both knew: a bored elf was a troublesome one.

Andor had at first protested against Nicholas's single restriction on his plan, but the saint had been adamant. "You will not engage in their wars as a fighter, Andor. If I find out you have, I'll send you back to Ljósálfrheimr where you can fight for your life against Dagrun and Alfr."

Andor had reluctantly agreed, and in the centuries that followed, he didn't take up a weapon as a warrior for someone else's war. That didn't mean he didn't take up a weapon or end up in war. Time, magic and curiosity had set him on many paths, and he learned many things. He'd been a battlefield medic, Bow Street Runner, wagon train scout, and a bodyguard. He pursued other occupations and vocations as well, some far more peaceful, like the current one as a preparator.

Humans lived short, intense lives, compressed into a handful of years the nearly immortal ljósálfr consider less than a breath of time. After almost ten centuries, he probably knew more about humans than any of his kin, and they still puzzled him mightily. He gazed at Claire, with her stiff posture and cool expression, and wondered what had made this previous child of magic into such a cynical adult.

"If you have lunch with me today, I'll pick up the tab," he said. "As far as the translations, I will be happy to help you regardless of your answer to my invitation."

She winced. "I'm sorta clumsy at this—"

He held up a hand to forestall the apology hovering on her lips. "It's fine, Claire." He liked the feel of her name on his tongue. "Have you been to Paulie's?"

Her eyes lit up. "Every chance I get. Great food."

They settled on a time to go. Claire gave Andor a small wave before she headed back to the lab. "See you in a couple of hours."

He inclined his head. "Claire." He watched her walk away, her long strides carrying her out of his sight in moments. A hint of the soap she used on her skin still lingered in the air, a touch of spring in autumn. A tide of heat in his blood.

CHAPTER FIVE

C laire was certain she'd made a terrible mistake. She could argue that asking Andor Hjalmarson for translation help had simply been a request rooted in the pursuit of professional efficiency.

A louder, more honest part of herself called bullshit on that.

And it was. While Andor's fluency in Armenian certainly came in handy in helping her with some of her provenance research, it had been a far more convenient way for her to spend time with and get to know him without every mentioning the dreaded, painfully awkward word "date."

A good plan, but it didn't take long for her to see the major flaw—Andor himself. Handsome, intelligent, well-read and charming without the arrogance and hubris that often came along with the positive traits, he seemed too good to be true. Claire entertained more than a few stray thoughts that she was meeting a serial killer for lunch or a man who harbored a secret, unnatural affection for livestock.

A week of lunch meetings every day blunted her paranoia but did a fine job of escalating the gossip among her co-workers. She shrugged off the sly glances and smiles that followed them anytime she and Andor met, whether for lunch, in a meeting or just passing in the halls. Once the rumor mill cranked up, it was hard to stop it. Trying to stop it just fueled the speculations, and she refused to feed that monster.

She succumbed to her own suspicious curiosity today. It was their fifth consecutive lunch meeting (she refused to call it a date), and Andor had driven her to a Vietnamese noodle house perched on the edge of downtown Houston that locals praised as having the best pho and banh mi sandwiches in the city. Andor placed their order in Vietnamese, surprising the woman behind the counter.

Unlike her, Claire no longer gaped at Andor. She had learned from their previous outings that he was fluent in several languages beyond Armenian. They placed their order, found seats at a table and settled into one of the easy conversations that had Claire trying not to check her phone or the clock on her PC every five seconds before lunch time.

At least that's what happened before this lunch. This time, Claire strangled two napkins into mangled wads of paper under Andor's curious gaze. "Can I ask you a question?"

His broad shoulders lifted in a shrug. "Of course." He sipped from his water glass.

"Have you ever killed anyone for fun or had an affair with a sheep?"

Andor sputtered and choked. His glass hit the table at the same time his knees knocked the underside in reflexive shock. The action rocketed the glass across the slick surface. Claire caught it in one hand, her quick reflexes the only things that saved her lap from an ice water dousing. She thrust one of the crumpled napkins at him. He snatched it and coughed into the crinkled folds until his eyes streamed tears and a flush reddened his face and neck. He motioned for his glass. She handed it back to him, wincing as he struggled for enough breath to sip the water and calm the cough. If he walked out right now and stranded her at the restaurant, she wouldn't blame him.

Instead, he wiped his eyes and leveled a baffled look on her. "No to both questions," he said between shallow gasps.

Claire didn't need to look in a mirror to know the heat blooming on her face turned her as red as Andor. She didn't know which was the worse blush—hers for mortification or his for near-asphyxiation of which she was the culprit.

"I'm so sorry," she said. "That came out wrong."

"That came out odd." Andor took a cautious swallow of water. "I don't think I can imagine a way such a question might come out right."

He had a point. Claire sighed and prayed her effort to dig her way out of this self-created awkwardness didn't end up digging her deeper. "Gossip is flying left and right at work. Everything from us having wild monkey sex in one of the supply closets..."

If her cheeks grew any hotter, she'd combust. "To you being a psychopath living the double life of a nice, handsome museum preparator while keeping your mom's mummified corpse in your attic."

Andor's eyebrows had slowly ratcheted up his forehead during her recitation, accompanied by an ever-widening smile. By the time she finished, he wore a full grin. "And where does the sheep come in?"

"That's just the icing on the cupcake." No way would she admit to the sheep conjecture.

The server's arrival with their food delayed his response. They spent the next few minutes in silence, Claire doctoring her pho; Andor taking bites of his sandwich.

"What do you think of the pho?" he asked her after she took a few sips and ate some of her noodles.

"Excellent." She dabbed her mouth with her napkin. "You have amazing radar for places that serve good food." She didn't flatter. While they took turns picking up the bill—at her insistence—he chose the restaurant, and he chose well every time. Greek dolmades in lemon sauce, grilled tuna steak sandwiches with wasabi mayonnaise, ropa vieja with white rice smothered in black beans accompanied by a side of sweet plantains. Andor knew where to eat well and not break the bank for the indulgence. Accustomed to a quick lunch of a sandwich from home or a bag of chips from one of the vending machines near her cube, Claire had eaten better this week than in the past year.

She twirled a bundle of noodles from her soup bowl onto her chopsticks. Andor paused in wolfing down the second half of his sandwich and wiggled his eyebrows at her. "Don't tell me you pay attention to office gossip?"

Claire squeezed more sriracha sauce into her broth and stirred vigorously. "Not usually, but I've never been the center of it before, and it's driving me crazy." She looked up at him, her spoon halfway to her mouth, and paused.

A shaft of sunlight, partially guillotined by the aluminum blinds covering the windows, bathed the side of Andor's face, casting his profile in high relief. His was an aesthetic visage, beautifully constructed but unyielding, as if he'd been created from marble instead of clay, his creator a sculptor instead of a potter. The only nod to softness in his features was his mouth, with an upper lip as wide and generous as his lower one. A mouth that smiled easily and often. Surely, whoever first wrote the definition for sensual kissing was inspired to do so after they kissed someone with a mouth like that.

"Such deep thoughts, Claire. What's going on in there?"

She blushed and spooned soup into her mouth to keep from answering right away. "Sorry to startle you with my weird questions."

Andor grinned. "To answer both, I've never killed anyone for fun, nor have I harbored an unhealthy fascination for anything remotely ovine."

Claire waved her spoon at him. "That's good. You don't live in your mom's basement and keep her mummified corpse in a rocking chair, do you?"

"No. I live in a garage apartment that I rent from a landlord named Sal Hopkins. He looks nothing like my mother, who, as far as I know, is alive and well. And while I've experimented in different professions, mummification hasn't made it to the list yet."

His levity faded. "If the gossip disturbs you that much, Claire, we don't have to meet. I'm at the Carmichael temporarily. You work with these people long-term. I don't want to cause you problems."

The thought of no more outings with this lovely man soured the soup in her stomach. She put down her spoon. "Don't be silly. Just because I'm not used to being the focus of gossip, doesn't mean I'm going to let it dictate what I do. Besides, this is fun." She gave him an uncertain look. "Are you enjoying it?"

Tiny flames kindled in Andor's eyes. "Very much. I want to keep meeting, even if you have nothing for me to translate."

She'd have to be thick as a brick not to read his not-so-professional interest. Dread and anticipation brewed a roiling potion inside her. It had been a long time since she even considered courting a man's interest. She didn't want to get her hopes up and have them shattered later, and she had her son to consider in every dating equation. In her experience, few men were willing to entertain more than a couple of dates or a one-night stand with a woman who parented a special needs child.

She liked Andor—a lot—but lunch was all she'd be willing to risk, no matter how tempting the company.

They finished their lunch with a much more mundane but enjoyable conversation between them. Claire waited by the door while Andor left the tip. His hand on her back as he guided her out of the restaurant sent a pleasurable wave of heat through her body.

On their way back to the museum, Andor turned down the radio and asked the one question Claire hoped he wouldn't. "Have dinner with me tomorrow night."

She groaned inside, sick with disappointment. "I'm sorry. I must decline."

Chapter Six

Nearly a thousand years living in Midgard had not dulled Andor's fascination with humanity. The basic behaviors didn't change much over the centuries, a reason he believed history tended to repeat itself. Humans, however, were a curious, restless lot. The ljósálfar lived countless years, content to let one day, one year, one century remain the same as the many before it. Sometimes there were battles with the dökkalfar, sometimes with a jötunn bent on mischief, but the long lives of both light and dark elves were but ripples on the surface of a still pond compared to humans. Short-lived, contentious, often chaotic, humanity raced and lurched by turns through time, desperate to experience everything it dreamed before a Norn cut short its existence.

When he began his exile with Nicholas and moved among the men of Midgard, Andor had disliked the frenetic ignorance that seemed woven into the very fabric of the human spirit. His opinion changed over time. His kin would say he'd been corrupted or tainted by his long exile. Their verdict might be true. With his glamour in place and generations of experience behind him, he could easily be mistaken as a human—except for one small unconquerable puzzle. He'd never understand the minds and hearts of human women. Then again, from all the moaning and groaning he'd heard across centuries and countries from human males, that complaint was hardly a singular ljósálfar failure.

Andor smiled to himself. Claire Summerlad, the Sunday's Child who had captured his memory and forgotten her magic, proved to be exceptionally confusing. He didn't think he'd ever met a more guarded woman, human or ljósálfar, and he'd courted many of both during his life.

Their lunch dates, initiated by him to satisfy his long-standing curiosity about her, had become something far more. He watched the clock for the noon hour, his eagerness to see her palpable in the rising beat of his heart and the restlessness in his limbs. The job at the museum kept him interested and busy, but always, always, Claire's elegant features and rare smile lingered in the back of his mind.

Reserved and business-like during their first lunch meeting, she had slowly opened to him as he helped her translate documents from Armenian to English and joked that some of the commentary in the margins of a few manuscripts she'd researched were anything but religious.

She didn't bring her laptop for lunch date number three, and he didn't ask. They spent a too-short hour chatting of inconsequential things—favorite movies, favorite food, favorite songs. She was far more fascinating than research notes on medieval hymnals. During lunch number four she spoke briefly about her son Jake.

Andor recalled that part of their conversation, short as it was.

"I overheard you tell Delilah yesterday you had to pick up Jake. Your son?" He crossed his fingers in his lap and hoped Jake wasn't a boyfriend or even worse, a husband.

Claire nodded, a softness entering her eyes along with an odd wariness. "He's ten. I have a baby-sitter look after him once school is out and until I get home."

She said nothing else about her son after that. No stories of childhood antics, sports events or personality quirks. No bragging of grades or tales of trips to friends' houses. Just his name, his age and the fact he had a babysitter who watched him after school. Andor wanted to ask more, but the look in her eyes warned him he'd get nothing else. He smoothly switched subjects and watched, confounded, as she visibly relaxed.

He thought a few meetings and a few conversations would satisfy his wonderings about Claire. His interest would wane, and he'd move on to his next flight of fancy before Nicholas called him to his annual duties. Instead, his interest had deepened to fascination then to enchantment as he came to know the woman who'd first captured his attention one Christmas past.

When he invited her to dinner, Andor had been sure she'd say yes. Cautious and reserved she might be, but she had expressive eyes, and he hadn't mistaken her attraction to him. She accepted every invitation to lunch. So when she declined his invitation to dinner, Andor felt like he'd been sucker-punched. He'd grown overconfident, saw an interest that wasn't there and made wrong assumptions.

He was good at hiding his emotions, but it took effort to relax his hands on the steering wheel as he drove back to the museum after lunch. "May I ask why?"

Claire fiddled with her purse strap, her gaze alighting briefly on his face before flitting away. "I won't be able to get a babysitter for Jake on that short of a notice."

Was that it? Not an insurmountable obstacle, and the tightness in his chest eased. "You can bring him with you," he said. He wanted more time with Claire, and if that included her son, so be it. Her child was a part of who she was. Besides, after ten centuries of acting as Santa's bodyguard, delivery boy and overall helper, he'd grown to like human children. They saw magic in everything. "I'd like to meet him. He can even pick the restaurant."

Claire's shoulders sagged a little, her faint smile rueful. "Thanks, but that won't work. Jake's not…" She trailed off, her gaze drifting to some point in a middle distance he couldn't see. A frown creased her brow for a moment before smoothing away, and her back straightened. Andor didn't miss the sudden death grip she held on her purse strap. "We can have dinner at my house if you want."

Judging by the look of dread on her face, he was sure he'd misheard her. She looked like she just invited him to a public hanging, and she was the condemned.

"An excellent idea," he said before she changed her mind. Something warned him—a flicker in her eye, the twitch of her eyebrow maybe—this was more than just another alternative to dinner out on a Friday night; it was a test of some sort.

Andor mentally shrugged. So what. A dinner, a hanging; he was fine with whatever she planned. He'd either end up helping her wash dishes or saving her from the noose. He was quite capable of doing both. "I'll bring the food. Just tell me the time and what you two want to eat." He waited, hoping she wouldn't rescind the offer.

She uncurled her fingers from around the purse strap—a good sign. "How about 7:30? Don't worry about Jake. He's a picky eater. I'll have something for him at home."

They pulled into the employee parking lot. Andor found a parking spot but kept the car running a moment longer. "What should I bring for you?"

"Surprise me." Claire smiled, opened her door and unfurled her tall frame from the seat. Andor unapologetically admired the view for a moment before killing the engine and joining her on the walk back to the building.

He escorted her to her cube, greeted a slyly grinning Delilah—he'd never think of her as Dee—who had peeked around the corner of the wall separating her cube from Claire and left with a brief promise to see Claire the next evening. His sensitive ears caught the follow-up conversation between the two women.

"Sooo, how was lunch?" Delilah's voice rang sing-song down the hall, followed by Claire's more exasperated "Not another interrogation."

"I just asked how lunch was."

"Yeah, and then you ask me how he licks his spoon and if I've seen him naked yet."

Andor held in his laughter until he made it to the loading dock, certain Claire wouldn't appreciate his amusement.

He spent the following day, thinking of Claire's fleeting smile while he and two other preparators wrapped and packed the fragile ceramics that would be shipped to another museum for exhibition in New Mexico. Evening couldn't come fast enough, and after a quick text message from her at the end of the day assuring him they were still on for dinner, Andor bolted from the museum.

Now, at 7:30 on the dot, he stood at the door of a small home fronted by a modest porch with a swing on one side and potted plants on the other. Claire answered the door on his second knock. Dressed in a black blouse and jeans that highlighted the length of her legs, she stood within the golden corona cast by the porch light, as beautiful and luminescent as any ljósálfar woman under moonlight.

"Sunday's Child," Andor said softly.

Her eyebrows rose. "Pardon?"

He held up two bags of fragrant take-out. "You said surprise you. I brought Indian."

She gave a delicate sniff, and her eyes widened. "That smells marvelous. Come in!" She directed him to a modest table set in a part of a main room designated as a dining area. The table was set for three. A votive candle sat in the middle alongside a bud vase holding two carnations.

Andor set his packages down and turned to survey the room. Small and modest, the living room/dining room combination reflected Claire's muted tastes. The colors, the lighting and the furniture gave a sense of peace and calm, along with an unspoken invitation to have a seat, prop your feet up and stay for a while. Even the music, played low, and piped softly through speakers against one wall added to the home's cozy ambience.

Claire's gaze rested heavily on him. "Welcome to the manor. Not grand, but it's home."

He'd lived in soaring palaces built of starlight and gemstones, where moonbeams striking the water spilling from fountains resonated like the chime of exquisitely tuned bells. He preferred this. "I like it. It feels like a sanctuary from a hard day."

Her entire demeanor eased, and her wide smile deepened the tiny lines at the corners of her eyes. "Thanks. That's a lovely thing to say." She gazed at him a moment longer before giving a start. "I'll get Jake. I told him we were having company tonight."

She disappeared for a moment into a short hallway, returning with a young boy who clutched a tablet in one hand.

Dark-haired where his mother was blonde, Jake had inherited her refined bone structure and arched eyebrows. His gaze was focused on the tablet screen, and he didn't look up when Claire nudged him closer to Andor. "Jake, this is my friend Andor. Say hello."

"He-wo." Jake's gaze flickered briefly to his mother, but he still didn't look at Andor, and his greeting sounded…young, the vowels broad and the consonants blunt as if spoken by a toddler instead of a ten-year old.

Andor crouched down to eye level with the boy. He didn't hold out his hand to shake, suspecting he'd get no response. "Good to meet you, Jake. I work with your mom at the museum. She's amazing, but I bet you already know that." He glanced at Claire, whose cheeks had gone rosy at his compliment, and winked.

She patted Jake on the back. "Go sit at the table, please. We're about to eat." He did as she instructed without protest or any verbal response at all. Claire's eyes were shadowed, the wariness returned full force in both her gaze and her posture as she turned to Andor. "Jake's autistic," she said softly. "So don't be too weirded out if he does odd things at the table while we're eating. You're a stranger, and having someone over for dinner who isn't the babysitter is out of routine. He might act out."

Andor watched Jake sing to himself, a wordless tune. The boy rocked in his chair, occasionally flicking the back of his neck with his fingers. "This is why he couldn't go out with us?"

"Yeah. I don't keep him trapped at home all the time, but a loud, crowded restaurant on a Friday night would be a nightmare of overstimulation for him. See how he's snapping his fingers against his neck? That's stimming behavior, a coping mechanism he uses when something is out of the ordinary."

The fabric of her blouse was smooth across his fingertips where he touched her elbow. "He's a lot more polite about it than I would be. Usually by the end of dinner in a noisy restaurant, I'm ready to stab someone with my fork." Andor winked at Claire once more. "Yours is a better idea. Nicer place, better music, great food, and I won't have to shout at you across the table to be heard. And I was able to meet your son."

One graceful eyebrow rose. "Are you sure you're not a psychopath?"

He laughed. "Stabbing someone with a fork in an eating establishment would get me not only jail time but probably a mental health evaluation. That being said, I can assure you I'm harmless."

That wasn't true in many contexts, but Claire was infinitely safe with him. He protected what he cherished. The thought brought him up short. How had this woman—once a child blessed with magic now lost—embed herself so quickly and so deeply into his soul?

Something of that breath-stealing realization must have revealed itself in his expression. Claire's eyes widened. "Hey, you okay? You just went pale."

He nodded, still trying to recapture his mental footing. "I'm fine. Just hungry. We should eat. Passing out on your floor isn't how I want either of us to remember our first dinner together."

Dinner started out an exercise in endurance. At first tense, nervous and obviously resigned to the idea Andor would bolt for the door the second her son did something odd, Claire had given lengthy explanations for everything from why Jake could synchronize two separate videos on his tablet to play the exact thing at the same time but couldn't easily handle a fork to eat to how he used a particular program to help him communicate.

"He's echolaic too," she explained. "So if you say something, and he repeats a portion back to you, it isn't mockery."

Andor laid his hand over hers, feeling the twitch of her slender fingers against his palm. "Claire. Relax. I'm not a therapist; this isn't an interview for either you or Jake. It's just dinner. He's fine. I'm fine, but I'll take another beer if you have an extra."

It was a not-so subtle ploy, but she grasped it like a drowning person clutching a lifeline. "Of course! I'll be right back."

The kitchen was no more than five steps from the dining area and separate by a wall, but Andor guessed a few seconds away from the table would give her a little time to breathe. He glanced at Jake whose fingers flew over the tablet's screen, opening videos and games and closing them just as fast, as if the brief flashes of pictures they presented were far more entertaining than the content in its entirety.

"Jake, can I hear that song you played earlier from the two videos?"

Jake didn't look up, but his fingers danced across the screen, opening up files faster than Andor could track. Soon the two videos played together in perfect synchronization.

"Well done, child." Andor toasted him with his empty bottle. His heart stuttered in his chest when Jake suddenly looked up to meet his gaze. His face, still soft and rounded with youth, grew animated for a moment. "Elf," he said. His eyes returned to his tablet as if Andor had suddenly winked out of existence.

Andor gawked at Jake for a moment before breaking into a grin wide enough to squint his eyes shut. Claire had passed her gift of the deep sight onto her child. Jake, who didn't speak or hold a fork easily, could see the ljósálfar elf sitting at his mother's table.

Ah, Nicholas, he thought. Did you ever meet this boy on Christmas Eve?

Claire returned to the table, two bottles in her hand, her equilibrium restored. She gave him and Jake a puzzled look. "What were you two up to while I was in the kitchen?"

Andor clinked his beer against hers. "Plans to conquer the world. Jake will be my general."

The remainder of dinner was a far more lighthearted affair. Claire told stories about the Carmichael and some of the exhibit catastrophes that had turned the museum director's hair prematurely white. "I keep waiting for some of the exhibits to come alive at night, like in those films. I'm just afraid our security team would shoot first and ask questions later."

Andor regaled her with tales of his travels. His only permanent point of place, where he was required to appear annually, existed in another realm. When he wasn't at Nicholas's service, he lived a mostly nomadic existence in Midgard and had traveled its realm many times over. Claire listened wide-eyed as he described the places he had visited for days or weeks, sometimes a month or two before moving on.

Jake had grown tired of their company during Andor's recitation and disappeared into his room with the ever-present tablet. Andor adopted a crestfallen look. "I think I bored him."

Claire chuckled. "Unless you can sing the song "Hot Potato" six hundred times in a row, he probably won't find you that interesting. I, however, am hooked. If I hadn't heard you speak at least four different languages myself, I'd think you were trying to feed me a load. Have you really been to all those countries?"

"Every one." He didn't mention he'd visited most of them multiple times across the centuries, seen them rise, fall, change names, change governments, change religions. He went for the mundane instead, something Claire's practical thinking would accept. "It's doable if you're very wealthy or willing to work any odd job for the travel money."

"I imagine you have a very interesting resume."

Andor choked back a laugh. "An understatement, trust me."

After dinner, he only had to help her throw away cartons and load the dishwasher instead of rescue her from certain death. Claire made coffee, and they took their cups out to the back patio. The bench set in the middle of the plain concrete pad was just big enough for two and face out to a back yard fenced from the neighbors. Claire's hip was warm where it pressed against Andor's. He wished this was more than just the awkward first date, and he could stroke the length of her long thigh through her jeans.

Early November in Houston was one of the best times of the year. Cool enough to feel a snap in the air, but the mosquitoes that made a meal out of everyone during summer and early fall were gone. The dark silhouettes of two live oaks spread even darker shadows across the ground. Through the gaps between their branches, the sky wheeled salted with stars and clear of clouds.

Claire pointed up. "You don't see that too often. It's either a humid haze or light pollution that blots those out. One day I'd like to take Jake out to the George Ranch observatory. If I can coax him to look through a telescope, he can see the Milky Way."

Andor glanced behind him at the partially open back door. "Will he be okay in there?"

She nodded. "Until last year, I couldn't turn my back for a second, or he was in to something or destroying it. Imagine the terrible twos lasting for seven years." She snapped her fingers. "Then it stopped all of a sudden. I don't know if an internal light bulb came on or what. I didn't dissect it, just counted my blessings." Her gaze followed Andor's to the door. "He might join us in a little bit. He likes to watch his shadow move. In the summer, before the mosquitoes get too bad and the city starts to spray, we'll come outside and he'll follow fireflies."

Andor could hear it in her voice, a joy tinged with melancholy, at her son's antics. Claire chose to see the wonder in Jake's reactions to such things as his shadow and fireflies. Her deep Sight might be gone, but Andor had been wrong. She still saw magic, just a different, very human kind.

"Where is Jake's father?"

For a moment, she stiffened next to him, and her face tightened. "In Germany on business I think." She glanced at him from the corner of her eye. A rueful smile hovered on her mouth. "I know what you're asking. We divorced four years ago. We were only married for five. Bad choice on both our parts. Special needs children can be tough on even the strongest marriages. Ours was already in trouble. For Lucas, I think Jake's diagnosis felt like the key that locked him in a prison. He served me with divorce papers two months later."

Andor scowled. Lucas sounded like an idiot. "Who'd leave a woman like you and the child you made together?"

"That's very sweet of you." Her blush darkened her face, even in the moonlight.

He shrugged. "It's true."

She fiddled with the handle of her coffee cup. "It's tempting to demonize him, but he isn't a bad person, and I'm no saint. I have custody of Jake, and Lucas has visitation. He pays child support on time, every time. Not a dead-beat dad, just a distant one. I try to encourage him to spend more time with Jake, but honestly I think the autism scares him."

Andor frowned even harder. "He does know it isn't contagious, right?"

Claire chuckled. "He isn't quite that dumb. He's like a lot of people I guess. They avoid what they don't understand. Humans are odd ducks sometimes."

"No truer words," Andor said. He finished his coffee and set the cup down by his feet. "Do you miss him?"

The question earned him a full laugh. "Good God, no." She sobered a little. "That's not true. I miss having help with Jake or someone I can share a rant with when one of us has a bad day. An evening watching a show we both like. But that's less about the specific person and more about the perks of living with someone you love. Even when Lucas and I lived together, we rarely did the things I just mentioned."

He had nothing to relate to those moments she listed. They appealed to him greatly, made him wonder what it would be like to live a life waking up each morning with this woman in his arms, to spend evenings like this evening with her and Jake—not as a single date with the hopes of another to follow, but the expectation that the two would be waiting there, happy to see him when he came through the door.

It was such a human thing to crave. He'd been too long among them.

Andor rose from the bench and helped a startled Claire stand. "I have to call it a night, Claire."

Her features went blank, and her arms crossed in a protective gesture. "Was it something I said?"

It was everything she was and everything he wanted. The craving for her and the life he imagined with her left him reeling. He needed to get away, to think.

He grasped her elbows and tugged her closer to him. Her arms stayed crossed, a barrier between them. Light from the living room spilled from the open back door. He and Claire stood in the wedge of luminescence it cast across the patio.

"It was everything you said." Andor stroked her stiff shoulder. "It was how you looked, the way your house felt, the way Jake smiles."

She jerked in his grasp. Her eyes rounded. "Jake smiled at you?"

He caressed her other shoulder. "While you were in the kitchen." He didn't mention it happened when Jake called him an elf. "I want to spend the day with you tomorrow. Both of you."

Claire blinked. "But…"

"I'm leaving for the night, Claire. I'm not running away. There's a difference." Her shoulders loosened a tiny bit under his hands, though her arms remained crossed. "Besides, despite what you may think or how spineless Lucas might act, you and Jake just aren't that scary."

That made her laugh and drop her arms to her sides. "Oh well then, that's a game changer. And we worked really hard to be terrifying." She reached up to flatten her hands over his where they rested on her shoulders. "Sounds like fun. We're yours for tomorrow."

Her words sent a hot shiver of anticipation down his spine. Andor wanted to enfold her in his arms, kiss the soft mouth that smiled at him now. But he held back. One goodnight kiss wouldn't be enough, not for him.

They made plans to visit Hermann Park and the grassy hill above Miller Outdoor Theatre. Jake could enjoy the outdoors and open space where the noise was distant and people spread farther apart.

Before Andor left, Jake came out, and at his mother's coaxing, told him goodbye. Claire missed it, but Andor caught the flicker of the boy's gaze on him and the small upturn of one corner of his mouth, as if to remind Andor of the secret they shared between them.

Claire followed Andor out to the front porch. While he refrained from kissing her mouth, he did avail himself of her slender hands, raising both to his lips in a courtly gesture. "Thank you for dinner, Claire."

"You brought the food. I just provided the table and the microwave. I should be thanking you."

She kept her hands in his, and her eyelids dropped to half-mast over her eyes. The tip of her tongue peeked between her teeth to swipe at her lower lip. Andor inhaled sharply at her unconscious invitation. He leaned toward her. Such a sweet mouth, shaped to fit perfectly against his.

He pulled away and dropped her hands. Claire backed up a step, the sleepy look gone; her usual guarded expression in place. Andor bowed. "I'll see you tomorrow, Claire. Goodnight."

Her gaze on his back burned hot on his skin, but he didn't turn around as he strode down her walkway and slid into his car. She waved once and disappeared back into the house. Andor leaned his forehead against the steering wheel. The memory of a long ago conversation he'd had with Nicholas came back to him.

"I wouldn't want to be human. Such short lives in which to try and do something."

Nicholas tucked his pipe stem into the corner of his mouth. Wisps of smoke curled out of the pipe bowl, shaping themselves into stars and horses, sailing ships and planets. "Don't be so quick to judge, son. Forever is a notion. You can live it across centuries or in a single hour. It's how you choose to spend the time given."

At the time, Andor hadn't understood Nicholas's cryptic remark. He did now. A thousand-year exile of nomadic existence. One evening with Claire Summerlad. He had just glimpsed Forever.

CHAPTER SEVEN

C laire paused in logging information into the database that held the files on Dee's upcoming illuminated manuscript exhibit. "Dee, come look at this. Did you get documentation on this latest manuscript lot?"

The curator rolled her chair into Claire's cube and peered at the screen. A scanned copy of a manuscript filled Claire's monitor—An angel with black wings holding an unconscious or dead woman in his arms. An illuminated border of gold leaf and red pigment surrounded the illustration. Below it, flowing black script executed in a steady hand told a moral lesson on the incurring the wrath of a vengeful God.

Dee frowned at the screen. "I don't recognize that manuscript. It isn't from the Matenadaren lot."

Claire clicked several screens back and scrolled through a typed list. "No, private owner—anonymous. This is that lot Dr. Vecchio brokered for us. Remember? Thing is, I have nothing more on it or the other six manuscripts that came in with it. Just lot numbers and dates. No provenance, no point of origin, nothing."

"That's weird. Giovanni Vecchio is very meticulous. He's brokered stuff for us before, and we always get a mountain of information with the lots. Are you sure it wasn't scanned to another database?"

Claire tapped her keyboard. "Positive. I've checked and double-checked." She clicked back to the manuscript with the black-winged angel and then through subsequent files depicting more angels, some wielding swords, others on their knees begging for mercy. "These are markedly different from the Matenadaren group. Same style but the content is…it looks almost Enochian. When was the last time you saw an illumination depicting an angel embracing a woman like that?"

"Never." Dee's voice sounded thin and strained. Claire glanced up and caught an odd look on her friend's face. Terror, sadness, a strange yearning. The expression faded as quickly as it appeared, but for some reason, the fine hairs on Claire's nape stood on end. "You alright?"

Dee, still pale around the mouth, nodded. "Yeah, I'm good. Just wondering how I could have missed that gap. I'll e-mail Vecchio to see what's up. Probably won't hear from him until after the holidays. I think he's visiting family in Italy.

Claire gave an appreciative whistle. "Must be nice."

Dee's voice had lost its strain, returning back to the teasing tones with which Claire was familiar. "Which one? Family or Italy?

" Italy of course." Family was nice too. Claire's was very small. Just her and Jake. But the holidays in Italy? Maybe one day—when she won the lottery.

"Invitation still stands if you want to come to my parents' place for Thanksgiving." Dee wheeled her chair back to her cube. "Mom promised she wouldn't serve the turkey raw this year."

Claire laughed. Dee's mom was notorious for her epic culinary failures. "Thanks, but Jake couldn't handle a combination of strange place, strange people and noise for several hours. Besides, I have company that day."

The words were barely out of her mouth before Dee zipped back into her cube. "I'm not much of a betting person, I but I'd lay money down company is the hot preparator you're attached at the hip to these days."

Ignoring the suggestive eyebrow wiggle Dee gave her, Claire sniffed. "Maybe."

Dee disappeared behind her cube wall once more. "I'll want details."

Claire rolled her eyes. "You always want details."

Andor had accepted her invitation to Thanksgiving dinner two days earlier. Claire had set herself up not to be disappointed, fully expecting him to decline for any number of reasons—family out of town, another commitment with friends. She didn't even want to imagine he might spend the holiday with another woman. Claire had no claim to him. She had lunch with him almost every day, and he visited her house for dinner several times a week. They'd even made it to the symphony once and a play, with Elise threatening to kill her if she called the house twenty times to check on Jake.

"Don't even think about it," the babysitter warned. "I know my job. You know I know my job. Jake and I will have fun eating all the toppings off the pizza and watching Total Drama Island. Have fun. Stay out late. You won't be missed."

She closed the front door on Claire and Andor and turned off the porch light. Claire had glanced at Andor. "Elise is a little blunt."

"And obviously very capable," he said. "I like her, especially her eyebrow piercings."

While Claire couldn't imagine how Andor might be seeing someone else when he spent so much time with her, she was far too fearful of engaging her heart more than it already was by assuming they were now a couple. He hadn't mentioned it; neither had she. Hell, they hadn't even kissed yet, something she hoped to remedy very soon.

When lunch time rolled around, she left the office space she shared with Dee and sought out Andor. She found him in one of the lower-level workrooms. The screeching blast of a multiple power saws cutting wood made her clap her hands to her ears. She spotted him in one corner of the room, ripping boards on a table saw. He wore a long-sleeved sweater that hugged his torso, delineating muscle and the width of his shoulders. His hair was tied back in its usual queue, and he'd donned safety lenses and ear muffs while he worked.

Claire waited by the door until he finished ripping a board. She didn't want to wave and distract either him or the two other preparators working at the saws. He glanced up, saw her and shut the saw down. Claire motioned she'd wait for him in the hallway.

The hall was silent as a crypt compared to the noise in the workroom. Andor emerged, sans ear muffs and lenses. His slow smile warmed her down to her bones. "Hello, Claire."

She liked that he didn't address her as "babe" or "beautiful" or the numerous terms of affection so many people used. Claire didn't have a problem with them per se. While she and Lucas were still married, she often called him "babe." But Andor had a way of uttering her name as if he savored something sweet, letting it glide slowly off his tongue to breathe across his lips. Never had she been so glad to bear that simple, one-syllable name.

The chilly hallway had suddenly grown stifling. She plucked at her sweater and returned Andor's smile. "Working through lunch today?"

He glanced at the clock on the opposite wall. "That time already?" Regret darkened his eyes to cobalt. "I'm afraid so. We're building the display bases for the gala decorations so we can just snap them together and move them when the designer says it's time."

"The Ainsley Hall is gorgeous already. I can't imagine how much more you can add for the gala."

She'd stood in wonder along with the rest of the employees and gawked at the miracle the preparator and design teams had wrought. The Carmichael always created a holiday exhibit of huge trees decorated with ornaments from cultures around the world as well as themes based on movies, history and literature. Preparators and designers worked through the day and night to complete the exhibit, unveiling it first in the early morning hours to the rest of the staff. Andor had given her a bow at her applause, the only hint of fatigue from a laborious all-nighter, the faint shadows under his eyes.

"Are you going to the gala?" His gaze searched her face.

Claire sighed. "Not if I could help it, but it's mandatory that staff goes. So I have a too-expensive dress that I'll wear once hanging in my closet, along with a pair of heels guaranteed to cripple me by the end of the evening. I just hope the caterer doesn't serve cardboard chicken and cold asparagus." Bad food used to not bother her. Andor was turning her into a picky gastronome.

"What about you?" she asked. "You're on loan to us, so I'm guessing you don't have to go if you don't want to." She crossed her fingers behind her back, hoping he would go. Hoping he'd go with her.

"That depends."

"On what?"

One eyebrow arched, along with his smile. "If I'm invited."

Claire's heartbeat jumped. She could feel her pulse thrum in her neck. "You haven't gotten an invitation yet? A handsome guy like you?" *Please say no. Please say no.*

Surely it was illegal for a smile to have that much power over someone. "Not one. At least not the one I want."

"Maybe I'll invite you."

They were suddenly no more than inches apart from each other. Andor's breath ghosted across her forehead and hairline. "I'd be very interested in that invitation," he said softly.

She touched his arm, the hard bicep flexing against her fingers. "Do you dance?"

"Invite me and find out."

Claire was cautious; she wasn't stupid. "Would you like to go to the benefits gala with me next month?"

Andor leaned down, and Claire's eyes closed at the sensation of body heat, the smell of sawn wood, and the cool winter scent clinging to the sexiest shirt she'd ever seen on a man. "Ah Claire, I thought you'd never ask."

Thanksgiving dawned overcast and cold with the threat of rain. Claire had risen when it was still dark outside to start dinner preparations. She was an adequate cook, but for four years, she'd only had to cook for herself and Jake. Chicken tenders and fish sticks for him, spaghetti, salad in a bag, or the occasional pan-grilled steak for her didn't exactly expand her culinary skills. She prayed her efforts today wouldn't see Andor driving them to 24-hour greasy spoon just to get an edible meal.

Andor arrived at noon. Claire met him at the door holding a chef's knife in one hand. He backed up a step and held up a bottle of wine. "Surely, a Beekeeper Old Vine Zin can garner me some mercy."

Claire huffed a strand of hair out of her face and waved him inside. "I'm glad you're here."

He eased passed her, gaze steady on the knife. "I can see that."

She chuckled and gestured for him to follow her into the kitchen. Andor paused when he saw Jake sitting at the table winding and unwinding a skein of yarn around his hand. "Hi, Jake. Have you been helping your mom?"

Jake didn't look up from his task, but he smiled a little and without any encouragement from Claire said "Hi, Dor."

Claire almost dropped the knife. She choked back an excited yelp and glanced at Andor. He set the wine on the table and crouched near the boy but not so close as to crowd him. "Have you been helping your mom with Thanksgiving dinner?" This time only silence met his question, and Claire answered.

"He cleaned off the table and helped me set it."

Instead of ruffling Jake's hair or patting him on the shoulder, Andor knocked gently on the table. "Good job, Jake. That's a nice thing to do for your mom."

He stood and gave her a smile. "How can I help?"

She led him into the tiny kitchen, fragrant with the scent of herbs and roasted vegetables. All the counters except one were covered with an assortment of grocery supplies and pans. A turkey breast, still in its wrapping, rested in one pan near a cutting board layered with chopped vegetables.

Andor sniffed. "It smells good."

Claire scraped the vegetables into a waiting roasting pan. "Thanks. It's the stock for the gravy and a pan of dressing."

"Dressing?"

She mentally backed up. "Stuffing. This part of the country, we call it dressing." She paused. "Is this your first Thanksgiving?" She sort of hoped it might. He couldn't compare her food to someone else's then.

He snagged one of the aprons hanging on a hook attached to the pantry door and tied it around his narrow waist. "No. It's my third. I'm still trying to decide if the bird they served at the last Thanksgiving I went to was actually a turkey or an ostrich. It was enormous." He cracked his knuckles. "Now, how may I act as sous chef?"

Trying not to gawk too much at how a man could look that sexy in an apron, she passed him a boning knife from her knife block. "I don't suppose you can de-bone a turkey breast?"

Much to Claire's lack of surprise, he could, and he was scarily efficient. "You were a butcher once, weren't you?"

Andor grinned as he tossed the bones into the trash. "For a little while."

Not only did he de-bone the turkey, he butter-flied it on her instructions, stuffed it with the roasted red pepper and goat cheese filling she'd prepared, rolled and tied it into a roulade, slathered it in duck fat and slid the pan into the oven.

They worked together, teasing each other about Andor's jack-of-all-trades skills and Claire's assurances that the poultry in the oven was definitely turkey and not emu. She left him in the kitchen whipping egg whites or stirring cranberries in a saucepan while she checked on Jake, took him for bathroom breaks and fed him snacks.

When the cooking was done and the table groaning with food, Claire surveyed their handiwork, propped her hands on her hips and grinned at Andor. "We make a good team."

His smile wasn't as wide but far more intense. "Yes, we do."

That euphoric tide that always rushed through her every time he complimented her or even stood near her, struck her again. Stronger this time. Harder. It left her tongue-tied for a moment. She tried for a lighthearted response instead of the one she really wanted to give. "I still have a hard time believing you're not married or in a relationship."

As quickly as that rush of joy struck, it abandoned her at Andor's suddenly grim expression. What had she said?

"I'm not married, Claire," he said softly. "I do consider myself in a relationship." Those blue eyes burned like gas flames. "With you."

Claire clutched the serving spoon she held in a death grip. Her "you do?" came out as an incoherent squeak. She tried again. "You do?" He nodded. "But you haven't even kissed me yet."

The hard angles of his face softened. The faint smile returned. He wrested the spoon from her and set it on the table. Claire's "ohhh niiicce" made him chuckle into her hair as he slid his arms around her and pulled her tightly against his body.

He bent his head and Claire inhaled sharply as he nuzzled her neck just below her ear. Powerful shoulders flexed under her hands. "Patience, Claire," he whispered. "I will kiss you, and when I do, I won't stop with a kiss." Deep laughter tickled her ear. "Or maybe I will, but it will be the last of a thousand, along with all the caresses that will accompany them."

Her knees gave out, and she sagged in his arms. Andor caught her up, one hand sliding down to cup her butt. "Don't faint," he teased.

"It's more like I'll combust," she countered in a strangled voice. Her body was on fire. If Jake wasn't there and likely to walk in the room any minute, she'd wrap her legs around Andor's waist and demand he carry her to her bedroom. Forget Thanksgiving dinner.

She twined his ponytail around her hand instead and kissed his neck in the same place he'd tickled hers. He groaned at her touch and squeezed her harder. "I'm not very patient," she said.

Andor slowly peeled her off him, his breaths shallow and a blush riding the high ridges of his cheekbones. His eyes had gone that same cobalt color she'd seen earlier. "Call it Neanderthal or anti-quated, but I don't want to share you with someone else, Claire."

Her cheeks heated at that. "Not a problem, since you're the only guy I've dated in almost three years."

"I want to be the only one for the next twenty."

Claire hoped she didn't have a coronary brought on by sheer excitement. "That's rather fickle of you, don't you think?" She winked and was rewarded with Andor's deep laughter. She gave his arm a light stroke as she passed him on the way to the bedrooms. "Get the wine; I'll get Jake. While we're growing hot, the food is growing cold."

Dinner was a feast, and Claire was certain she'd be eating enough leftover turkey to sprout feathers. And that was after she sent most of it home with Andor. The weather outside had gone from dreary to miserable, with a steady drizzle making a murk of the last bit of daylight. A damp cold hung in the air, defying every attempt to layer up and keep it from seeping through clothing and skin. Claire disliked such days when she had to get out in it to go to work or run errands. Today, however, she loved it. Her house was warm and smelled of coffee and pumpkin spice. She sat on her comfortable couch, sandwiched between Jake who played his favorite game Dumb Ways to Die, and Andor, whose acerbic commentary about Santa's outfit in the movie they were watching on TV made her laugh.

"I hate that red leotard. Nicholas was a bishop. He would have worn vestments."

Claire gave him a puzzled side-eye and tried not to nestle too hard against the arm wrapped around her shoulder. Who knew someone got that worked up over a Santa suit? "I thought it was a Kriss Kringle thing. It's not?"

"No. Kriss Kringle is the Anglicization of the Austrian and German word Christkindl. The red suit is a modern element. Saint Nicholas is a lot older than that. A bishop of Myra, now Demre in Turkey. He was Greek. Some called him Nicholas Wonderworker or Nikaolos ho Thaumaturgos. He's the patron saint of sailors, children and pawnbrokers."

Claire almost choked on the coffee she just swallowed. "Are you serious? Santa protects pawn shops?" Somehow that just didn't fit with jolly, merry and Ho, ho, ho.

Andor expression was enigmatic as he stared at the TV screen. "Saint Nicholas is a lot more interesting than the rotund man we think of now in the red suit."

"I'll say. I'm guessing you came by your Santa knowledge while working on an exhibit?" God knew she'd stumbled across all kinds of bizarre and interesting things during her research projects.

Andor danced around her question. "You're an archivist. I'm sure you've discovered unusual things in your research.

Claire casually slid one hand over Jake's ear and nestled him close to her side to muffle his other ear. He'd put up with that for all of four seconds, so she spoke fast. "Oh, yeah. So I guess when I say I don't believe in Santa, I need to qualify that since he did exist."

Something flickered in Andor's eyes. It spoke of melancholy and regret. "When did you lose your belief?"

She released a squirming Jake and shrugged. "I don't remember exactly. Later than a lot of kids. I think I might have been twelve."

"That is later. Most are younger."

That was true. She'd held onto her beliefs, even in the face of the cynical scorn dished out by her peers. Her certainty that Santa existed had been fueled by more than her mother's assurances. "I think it was because I had this really vivid dream of meeting Santa one Christmas Eve. I was sure it was real and that I was wide awake. He was standing by this sad little tree my mom bought at a garage sale. I loved that tree."

She frowned, clawing at the hazy memory of a childhood she'd put behind her long ago. "He was wearing long robes." She glanced at Andor, who no longer stared at the TV but watched her with a stoic face. "Bishop's vestments I bet. He was standing next to an elf. A really tall one wearing armor of all things." She shook her head. "I thought Santa elves were little like the Keebler elves. And they don't go in armed to the teeth." She was getting a headache and tucked the memory back into the recesses of her mind. "Then again," she joked, "if Santa is the patron saint of pawn brokers, he probably needs a bodyguard elf."

Her smile faded when Andor didn't return it, and his eyes had a faraway look. She really needed to stop making jokes. She sucked at it. Serious was more her speed. "When did you stop believing?" she asked.

He came back to her with the question. His tempting mouth curved into her favorite expression. "I haven't."

"Haven't what?"

"Stopped believing."

Claire eyed him suspiciously. "Really?"

"Really."

Andor was handsome, intelligent, funny and good with her son. He was also a little odd about all things Christmas. Claire celebrated the last. Finally. The guy wasn't perfect. She leaned into his side. "That's nice. I like that you believe in magic."

Andor's fingertips combed through her hair. "The world is filled with magic, Claire. Jake is proof of that. You just have to look a little deeper."

Claire was falling hard for him. Falling hard and fast. She almost broke the sound barrier at his words. She had chosen so badly with Lucas. Did she actually get it right this time with Andor?

Her cell phone's ringtone knocked her back into reality. She grabbed it off the coffee table. "Speak of the devil," she murmured. Lucas's name and phone number flashed on the screen. Andor muted the TV.

Claire answered on the third ring. "Hey Lucas."

"Hey yourself, gorgeous," her ex said. "Happy Thansgifing." He slurred the words, and Claire suspected Thanksgiving dinner had been a buffet of double martinis or several shots of expensive single malt.

She raised a staying hand as Andor stood. "You too, Lucas," she replied. Leave it to her ex to spoil a perfect evening. "Do you want to speak to Jake?"

"Yeah. Wanna wish him Haffy Thansgif."

Claire rolled her eyes. Jake was more articulate than this, and he had speech therapy three times a week. "Hold on, I'll get him." She pressed the mute button and grasped Andor's hand. "Do you have to go?"

He nodded, his fingers caressing her knuckles. "I have to stop at the museum and check a few things. We were having trouble with the lighting on three of the trees in the Christmas exhibit." He lifted her hand to his mouth. Claire made a strangled sound when she felt the tip of his tongue glide across her fingers. His gaze was gaslight blue, full of heat and promise. "You beguiled me into staying longer than I meant to, Claire."

"Sorcery," she teased.

"The best kind," he replied. "I'll see myself out." He released her hand, waved to Jake and gestured to the phone. "He'll wonder if you've forgotten him."

She watched him disappear around the corner of the short hallway, heard the front door open and close, and listened to his car back out of her driveway. "I did that the moment I met you," she said softly.

CHAPTER EIGHT

Every year, on December sixth, Andor joined the throng of worshippers who entered the Basilica of Saint Nicholas in Bari, Italy and found a pew near the back of the church where he sat beside its namesake. This year was no different.

Nicholas, dressed in the garb of a twenty-first gentleman, leaned over and whispered, "I wasn't sure you'd come."

Andor kept his gaze on the altar and the steady parade of people looking for places to sit. "You say that every year, and I'm here every year."

He'd balked at attending the saint's feast day the first twenty years of his exile. This was ground sacred to a deity whose existence he acknowledged but didn't worship. He was ljósálfar-born and sensitive to the warp and weft of the magic woven into the air and ground peculiar to Midgard. It pulsed in sacred wells, grass-capped kurgans and temples like these. In this church built in Nicholas's honor it resonated heavy in his bones, a power colossal beyond measure and ancient beyond comprehension. The first time he crossed the church's threshold, he'd nearly bolted outside. It had taken sheer will to hold his glamour in place and keep his feet planted on the floor.

Nicholas muttered near his ear again. "This year is quite different. Someone else occupies your time and thoughts."

"Spying on me?"

The saint gave an affronted sniff. "I'm also the patron saint of one wayward ljósálfar."

An elderly woman sitting on the other side of Nicholas leaned forward, glared at them both and made shushing noises.

Andor almost broke a rib trying not to laugh out loud at the idea of Nicholas ordered to be quiet by a congregant in a church built in his honor on a day that celebrated his sainthood.

A mortified Nicholas hastily apologized in Italian to the woman and motioned for Andor to follow him outside the church. Andor didn't need to be told twice.

Once outside, the elf glanced back at the church doors; they were closing, a signal that the mass was about to begin. "You're going to miss the mass."

Nicholas waved away Andor's concerns. "I'll attend the Thursday hymnals or an all-night vigil at one of the Eastern Orthodox churches. There's also the Departure celebration in the Coptic church on the nineteenth. You're welcome to attend that."

"Humans certainly throw you a lot of parties."

The saint sighed and offered a rueful smile. "I get a lot of requests for intercession."

Andor shifted restlessly, the rhythmic surge of power moving like high tide under the church steps, sending arcane vibrations through his legs. "What did you want to tell me that's so important, you'd miss the biggest celebration in your honor?"

"You found Claire again."

Andor frowned, sensing more to Nicholas's brief statement. "I did. And what strings did you pull to make that happen?"

Nicholas shook his head. "Not a one. I might suggest you look to your Norns for such machinations, but I'm a Christian bishop and believe something greater is at work there." He began to pace, and Andor's unease ratcheted up a good six notches. The saint was typically a calm, good-natured presence. "If you hadn't come, I would have sent for you. The queen has summoned you to audience at the Ljósálfar court."

Andor didn't think his spine would freeze any colder if someone had poured ice water down his back. His exile wasn't yet finished, yet Dagrun summoned him home. "Why? I still have a dozen years left to my exile."

Nicholas's pacing sped up. "I don't know, but I received a message from Ljósálfheimr. Dagrun and Alfr both want to talk to you.

The elf instinctively reached for the sword he no longer wore at his hip. "If Alfr wants my head, he'll have to fight me for it." He wouldn't surrender to his own execution without a struggle. He had too much to live for. One woman, one child. He'd slaughter his way across Ljósálfheimr if he must to stay alive.

"Peace, son." Nicholas laid a hand on Andor's arm. "I don't think you're being summoned to die."

Every muscle in Andor's body had gone tight, readying for battle. "When do we go?"

"Now, if you're ready."

❧

The royal palace was unchanged since he'd last seen it a thousand years earlier. The fact shouldn't have surprised him. A thousand years was merely a breath in time to the near-immortal ljósálfar. Yet, Andor paused before entering the soaring structure whose crystalline walls gleamed in the shifting, multicolored light from far-off Asbrú. The static sameness weighed down on him, a claustrophobic stillness that had watched time pass and never blinked. How had he ever lived in such stagnancy and not been driven mad by boredom?

Beside him, Nicholas cast an admiring gaze on his surroundings. "I will never adjust to how beautiful this palace is." He glanced at Andor. "Are you glad to be back?"

"No."

The saint's eyebrows climbed up his forehead. The king and queen's arrival forestalled any reply. Elf and bishop bowed before the ljósálfar monarchs who took their seats on the two great thrones set on a raised dais.

"Rise." King Alfr's single-word command formed icicles on the windows lining the throne room.

Judging by his tone, the king had not summoned Andor back to share ale and good company. Andor glanced first at the elf king. Tall and striking, he was an equal counterpart in appearance to his blindingly beautiful queen, except for the reptilian coldness she lacked. That alone had always made Andor's hackles rise anytime he was in his king's presence.

Dagrun spoke, her voice the sweetest music. Beside Andor, Nicholas sighed. "We have missed your presence at court, Andor." The king snorted and was ignored.

She was his aunt and his liege. And a thousand years earlier, she'd been his judge and savior. Andor loved her as much as ljósálfar could love each other and prayed that whatever spurred this unexpected meeting between them, it remained peaceful.

"I treasure your affection for me, my queen," he said.

She smiled, and where ice had hung on the windows at Alfr's voice, crimson roses grew and spiraled around the columns. "Nicholas tells me you've been exemplary during your exile with him."

Andor glanced at Nicholas who winked. "He has been a mentor of great wisdom." And unstinting patience for the elf under his charge.

"Do you regret the actions that sent you to him in the first place?" Alfr's serpent gaze did its best to strip the skin of Andor's bones.

He could say he didn't regret them in the least. Alfr's favorite concubine was a lusty *mara* between the sheets but hardly worth a thousand-year punishment. Midgard, with its joys and its struggles, its short-lived humanity that embraced chaos, pondered the existence of gods and strove to conquer the stars, had bound him in both heart and spirit. Those tethers had drawn tight and fast when he met Claire for the second time in her life and fell in love with her. He regretted nothing of his actions.

That long answer would see his head separated from his shoulders.

"Yes," he lied. "I regret them deeply."

Nicholas coughed and cleared his throat but otherwise stayed silent and kept his gaze on Alfr and Dagrun.

The king settled back in his throne, his approval of Andor's answer written in his posture and the relaxing of his mouth. He still made Andor's blood run cold. "I can be forgiving," he said. "You may return to Ljósálfheimr." His eyes narrowed. "My mercy isn't limitless. Another mistake like the first one, and death, not exile, will be your punishment."

Having offered his judgment, Alfr stood and strode out of the throne room. When Andor straightened from his bow, he discovered Dagrun still seated on her throne, watching him. She motioned him and Nicholas closer. "Welcome back, nephew."

Andor didn't want to come back. Not any longer. A decision loomed before him, one that would change the course of his existence. He'd pondered the question in the darkness when he was alone in the bare garage apartment he rented as simply a roof over his head while he stayed in Houston. Then he'd assumed he had another twelve years of exile. In human terms, it was a long stretch in which anything could change, and he'd grown to see time in the way humans did.

He'd forgotten that ljósálfar could be fickle in many ways, as quick to forgive as to punish. Alfr's anger had cooled a little sooner than anticipated, and his pardon had caught Andor off guard. He would have to leave Claire and never see her again. The thought made his chest burn and his stomach roil. If he stayed in Midgard, he'd sacrifice something just as important.

Andor inhaled slowly, exhaled just as slowly and made his choice. "You have my gratitude, Your Majesty, however; I have no wish to return to Ljósálfheimr."

Nicholas's robes sent a draft swirling up from the floor as he spun to gawk at Andor. Dagrun's surprise was less obvious—the twitch of her hand where it rested on the throne's arm.

"Why ever not?" she asked. The roses on the soaring columns began to wither.

Andor edged closer to the throne. "I've grown to enjoy Midgard and all it offers."

The queen's upper lip curled. "There is no comparison between Ljósálfheimr and Midgard."

"No, there isn't. They are too different, but exile has taught me the charm of other realms, and I am content in that one. I wish to stay."

Nicholas grasped Andor's arm. His dark eyes held both wonder and desperation. "Andor, because I move freely among men, you could too as my ward. It's a dispensation granted to you during your exile. You can't live them among them elfin and immortal now."

Andor nodded. "I know."

The saint's fingers dug into his bicep. "Do you understand what you're saying?"

"Yes."

"It isn't just Midgard, is it, Andor?" Dagrun had abandoned her throne to stand in front of her nephew.

Andor bowed to her. "No, my queen."

Where before her mouth had curled in contempt, it now curved in a knowing smile tinged with sadness. "I will hold you to exile a little longer so you may help Nicholas one final year. And to give you more time to consider your decision. If you don't return to Ljósálfheimr by the dawn of *Solis Invicti*, your grace will leave you. You will be mortal, human, and without magic. Our realm will be forever closed to you. You will age, and you will die."

Nicholas's eyes glistened with tears. "Andor."

Andor didn't share the saint's sadness or the queen's melancholy. The smothering dread that had draped itself on his shoulders the moment he crossed into Ljósálfheimr was gone, replaced by euphoria and a restless need to fly from here and return to the world and the woman he'd grown to love. He grinned at the saint. "Forever is a notion, Nicholas. You said so yourself."

CHAPTER NINE

C laire checked her appearance in the mirror one last time and pronounced herself ready. Andor was on his way to escort her to the Carmichael's benefits gala. The program in her purse had promised an enchanted evening of holiday fantasy among the Christmas exhibit in the Ainsley exhibit hall. Dinner, dancing, an open bar and most importantly, a silent auction. The last garnered a lot of money every year from the wealthy museum patrons who attended the gala and bid on luxury items from first-class trips to rare antiques.

She presented herself to Elise and Jake who sat at the dining table gluing pieces of felt to construction paper for an art project. Jake kept licking glue off his fingers, and what he missed, he rubbed in his hair. Elise patted him on the back. "Dude, it's bath time after this, or I'll be able to stick you to the wall."

She whistled when she saw Claire. "Damn, you are seriously hot in that dress."

Claire pivoted slowly, hoping she didn't wobble too much in the heels. "Look okay? No panty lines? Pulled threads?"

Elise wiped a smear of glue off Jake's cheek. The boy flashed a glance at his mother. "Hot," he said.

The two women laughed. Elise gave her another once-over. "You're good. Better than good. You look great." She covered Jake's ears with her hands. "Mr. Andor sex-on-a-stick is gonna be sporting a boner all night."

"Elise!" Claire laughed, secretly admitting to herself how much she hoped that was exactly what would happen.

The dress she wore was a classic formal black dress. Long-sleeved, with nude netting stitched in black lace across the collar bones, it hugged her body in sleek lines that ended in a short train. Both modest and sensual, it had appealed to Claire's sense of style and contrasted attractively with her hair and skin.

Her shoes were the work of Satan's minions. Created and engineered to cripple the wearer in the most painful manner, they made any pair of legs look fabulous and every dress look haute couture. Claire had promptly succumbed to temptation and sold her soul, as well as her arches, to the demon posing as a sales clerk in the shoe store.

When the door bell rang, Elise rose from her seat and pointed at Claire. "You just stand there and look—" She lowered her voice. "Fuckable. I'll get the door."

Claire shook her head. She adored Jake's babysitter, even if her word choice took her aback sometimes.

Andor's comments when he saw Claire mirrored Elise's admiration if not the verbiage. His gaze slid over her, slow as honey, hot as a bonfire. "I don't think there are enough of the right words in any language to describe how you look."

Claire blushed. "Good or bad will do fine."

"Sublime," he said simply.

"Thank you. I can say the same for you."

She could say a lot of things if she wasn't virtually tongue-tied with awe. A tuxedo worked like her Satan shoes. It made just about anyone look good. Andor, however, went beyond good, beyond striking or sublime to jaw-dropping beautiful. His features were too hard to be called angelic, unless one compared him to an archangel—that celestial warrior who engaged demons in battle. Preferably the ones who designed the shoes she wore.

He wore his hair in its usual ponytail, and the casual look somehow gave the formal tux more pizzazz and interest. It was positively criminal to look that lickable in a bowtie.

"Are you two going to stand there all night staring at each other, or are you going to your party?"

Elise broke the spell that held them in place. Claire grabbed her purse and shawl, kissed a sticky Jake on the forehead and listed off instructions and phone numbers to Elise for the fourth time."

The babysitter scowled at her. "Go away, Claire. Jake and I got this. We're going to decorate that height-challenged Christmas tree you bought, eat junk food and watch cartoons. I'll see you later."

Andor guided Claire out the door with a wink at Elise. Once inside the car, they fell into a comfortable silence. Andor drove smoothly through the snarl of traffic, steering with one hand while he sought Claire's hand with the other and entwined his fingers with hers.

Since Thanksgiving, they'd grown ever closer, touching constantly when they could capture a moment of privacy. A brief caress down her back, the glide of her hand along his shoulders. Claire didn't ask him to kiss her, though the delicious anticipation of knowing he would soon—and wouldn't stop there—sometimes made her break out in a sweat. He told her of his family, a mother and father with whom he wasn't close, a friend with whom he was. His travels had taken him all over the world, giving him a unique insight into people in general.

He was funny and affectionate but always respectful to her as if he sensed the wariness she was fast tossing to the curb. After her divorce, Claire had guarded her heart and her son against all comers. Except for one awkward, disastrous date six months after she'd reclaimed her maiden name, she had turned down every offer. Until Andor. She hadn't abandoned her caution entirely, but he'd found a way through her armor, worn her down like river water over stone, only so much faster. When he suggested they see each other exclusively, Claire had wanted to shout her joy from the rooftop of her house.

She lifted their joined hands to her mouth and kissed his knuckles before setting his hand on her thigh. They still said nothing to each other, but the tension in the car jumped, and Andor's eyes had gone the gaslight blue Claire now recognized as his desire for her manifested.

At the gala, they joined co-workers at one of the tables set up in the Ainsley hall. Thousands of fairy lights woven into the tall trees and strung through the garland wrapped around columns and pinned to stair banisters cast the room in golden light.

Servers passed out champagne and offered hors d'oeuvres to the guests. A string quartet played from an upper balcony, mix of Christmas and dance music. Claire looped her arm through Andor's as they left the table to circulate among the crowd. "I think you've been stripped naked at least a dozen times since we've walked through the door." She would have to be blind not to catch the admiring stares Andor received when they arrived, and even now as they navigated through clusters of guests. She was guilty of doing it multiple times herself.

Andor met her gaze, his expression grim. "I hope not. I'm wearing Scooby Doo boxers." His expression never changed, even when Claire's eyes widened, and she glanced automatically at his crotch.

"Seriously?"

He broke into a laugh and spun her so she faced him. "No." He captured her right hand and settled his other hand on her lower back. "Dance with me, Claire."

She stepped into his embrace, happy to hold onto his broad shoulders. "So you can dance."

"I told you, if you invited me, you'd find out. How brave are you?"

"Not very, but if you step on my toes I won't feel it. My feet have gone numb."

They glided across the room, Andor guiding her unerringly over the floor and around other dancing couples. Claire felt like she was flying. Only this was better than flying, better than breathing even.

They danced straight through four more songs, stopping only when the quartet changed tempo to something faster and less suitable for the waltz or the boston. Andor guided Claire to a semi-secluded alcove at the perimeter of the hall.

The heat pouring off him was matched only by the fire inside her. She caressed the side of his face, tracing the angles of his cheekbone and nose, the sharp line of his jaw. He turned his face into her hand, his lashes dark and thick on his cheeks as he closed his eyes and kissed her palm.

"Do you think anyone will notice if we make out right here?" Claire's other hand busied itself wandering under Andor's tux jacket to stroke his narrow waist and the contoured muscles of his back. She felt the curve of his smile against her palm before he raised his head.

"Probably. And if you didn't like office gossip before…" He trailed off, his teasing expression sobering. He traced the line of her spine and curve of her hips, leaving trails of fire on Claire's skin. "We can leave if you wish."

She could hear it in his voice, that subtle coaxing that almost beguiled her into saying yes. "I'd love to but we can't. We have to stay through the dinner."

"And eat the cardboard chicken." Andor drew invisible designs on her neck with a fingertip. Claire leaned into his touch with a sigh. "Let's go back to our table. At least the conversation with others will distract me."

Claire huffed and slid out of his embrace. "Speak for yourself." She intended to learn the shape of his upper thigh under the shrouded protection of the tablecloth."

His low chuckle seduced her as much as his touch did.

The dinner lasted for years. At least it seemed that way to Claire who, if she were ever asked, couldn't remember what was served on her plate. She ate a little, chatted with her co-workers, including Dee who often cast her and Andor knowing looks. And Claire played with Andor's thigh under the table.

When dinner ended, Andor rose, helped Claire out of her seat and wished everyone goodnight. The weight of a dozen curious stares followed them out of the hall. She didn't care.

The return trip home was as quiet as the one to the gala. Andor took his turn learning the shape of Claire's thigh through her dress, and Claire tried not to squirm in her seat at the electric sparks that shot through her body at his touch.

They stood close together at her door, Andor looming behind her. Claire turned to him, her heart pounding from a combination of anticipation and dread of his answer. "Will you stay the night with me?" *Will you stay a lifetime with me?*

He stared down at her for long seconds, his somber, handsome face dappled in shadow. "Yes," he said in a tone that made Claire believe he not only answered the question she uttered, but also the one she did not.

She fumbled the key in the lock until Andor took it from her and unlocked the door. Elise's surprise at their early return morphed into a sly grin. She gathered her purse and jacket as if racing to beat the ticking of a stopwatch. "Jake's passed out in bed. I left his tablet charging on the table, so he can reach it in the morning if he wakes up before you do." She waved as she sailed out the door. "Have fun!"

Claire locked the door behind her, tossing the key on the hall table along with her purse and her shawl. Andor stood in the middle of the living room, his gaze hot enough to scorch cement as he watched her.

"Do you want something to drink?" Her voice rasped like sandpaper, and she cleared her throat.

"No."

She pointed to the hall leading to the bedrooms. "I want to check on Jake. I'll be right back."

Elise had left the closet light on for Jake and the door cracked to allow a sliver of illumination into the room. The boy lay still beneath his covers, and didn't so much as twitch when Claire kissed his forehead and ran her fingers through his hair. "Goodnight, sweetie. I'll see you in the morning."

She found Andor as she left him, a beautiful statue gracing the middle of her living room. Claire grasped her courage with one hand and his hand with the other and led him to her bedroom.

Andor placed a hand on the door before she closed it. "Don't you need to listen for Jake?"

She pointed to a monitor, one meant to listen to an infant, set on a nightstand by her bed. "Got it covered."

He smiled and closed the door for her.

Claire raised her face to his. "Can I have that kiss now?"

Andor eased her into his arms. His lips brushed hers, the faintest touch. Once, twice. A little harder—a lot hotter—each time. He lifted his head, and Claire uttered a wordless protest. "That was two kisses."

She grasped his coat lapels and dragged him down to her. "You promised me a thousand," she said and nibbled at his lower lip, gratified by the deep groan her caress elicited. "Don't be stingy."

The memory of intimacy had dulled over time. Claire hadn't slept with anyone since her divorce from Lucas. Grief over her failed marriage, fear of being a single parent to a special needs child, moving to a different house, all the other smaller, but equally stressful details that had nearly overwhelmed her, pretty much killed her interest in pursuing a relationship, casual or otherwise.

Andor had changed all that, and the desire coursing through her now made her quick, clumsy and eager. He was as enthusiastic as she. Clothes were pulled away, regardless of snapped buttons or stretched seams, and thrown into the corner.

Andor kept his promise, kissing Claire until her head spun, his tongue slick and hot in her mouth; his teeth gentle as he nipped a path from her neck and across the top of her shoulder. His hands skimmed her body, cupping her breasts, learning the curves and slopes revealed when he'd peeled the dress off her, his eyes darkening at every inch of skin revealed until they were nearly black.

Claire returned his passion, muttering words of admiration between soft moans as she mapped him with her touch, beguiled by all that he was—sleek muscle and winter pine scent, his obvious affection for her and acceptance of Jake. She wished she'd met him sooner; she was profoundly grateful she knew him now.

They stumbled to the bed, unwilling to let each other go for a second. Andor made love to her amidst a tangle of sheets and the caress of shadows. Claire's soft moan echoed his deeper groan when he slid inside her. The thrust of hips, the bite of a harsher kiss, the grip of her knees on his sides as he rode her deep and hard: Claire reveled in all of it.

Her climax skated the edge of her senses, sparking every nerve ending until she bucked against Andor and cried out his name in a carnal prayer. He followed her, his hands clenching the sheets on either side of her head as he groaned his pleasure into her neck.

Their post-coital torpor didn't last long, and this time it was Claire who clenched the sheets in white-knuckled hands.

They lay entwined afterwards, sweaty and replete. The sheets had been kicked to the end of the bed, the comforter shoved to the floor. Claire outlined the slopes and valleys of Andor's face with a fingertip, tripping lightly over the high bridge of his nose before tracing the arch of his eyebrows. His beautiful mouth was swollen from her enthusiastic kisses, and he nipped at her when she ran her thumb across his lower lip.

She was tired and wonderfully achy, as if caught in a kind of carnal hangover. For all practical purposes, she should be ready to pass out. Her emotions had other ideas. Claire considered herself a woman possessed of a healthy sexual appetite, but she'd never been able to separate her emotions from physical intimacy. Sex never was, and never would be, casual for her. She gave her heart and her affection as well her body to her lover, and with this lover, she feared she'd just given her soul. The thought terrified her, and she batted it back to the corner of her mind. She refused to regret this night, or any other that might come after it. If it all ended in a broken heart, she would consider it worth the tears shed. Comfortably numb was no way to live.

Unaware of her inner turmoil, Andor slid a hand down the curve of her waist and swell of her hip, returning to her waist to repeat the same stroke over and over. His eyes were heavy-lidded and still more black than blue. "What do you want for Christmas?"

His question, asked while she struggled with her darker musings, made Claire stumble a moment. "Christmas?"

"Yes. Christmas. You know, that day of gift giving and such? It's a week away."

Except for the gift cards she exchanged with Dee each year, Claire didn't receive Christmas gifts. She bought a few for Jake—toys with textures that might appeal to his sense of touch, puzzles to help him remember colors and letters, an app for his tablet that made funny noises he'd listen to over and over and laugh at with every repetition.

You in my home; you in our lives. She wanted to say it but opted instead for the safer, more light-hearted answer. She grinned and wiggled her eyebrows suggestively. "Didn't I just get it?"

Andor didn't share her amusement. His face darkened, turned pensive. Claire reared back a little, suddenly frightened. She hadn't answered the way he hoped. That was obvious, but she didn't know what answer he wanted from her. She asked a question of her own. "What do you want for Christmas?"

He stared at her for so long, she wondered if he planned to ignore the question altogether. "I want you to love me, Claire. To share your life, and Jake's, with me. Not just this Christmas, but for every Christmas afterwards. For a lifetime."

The fact that she didn't physically shatter into a million tiny pieces at his words made Claire an instant believer in miracles. She blinked away the sudden burn in her eyes easily enough, but it took three tries to clear the tightness from her throat so she could speak.

She twirled a lock of his hair around her finger. "Is that it? I thought you were going to ask for something a lot more difficult to give—like a real shrunken head from the Aguaruna tribe or El Cid's Tizona sword."

She squeaked when his arms tightened around her hard enough to thin her breathing. Andor loosened his hold only a little. "I'm serious, Claire."

Claire's teasing grin faded. She cupped Andor's face in her hands and stared into a pair of eyes as blue as an ocean, and oddly enough, almost as ancient. "So am I." She kissed him, savoring his return kiss. "I will love you for a million lifetimes, Andor. Even into forever."

His expression changed, turned beatific as if he'd been lit from within. He rolled them across the bed until Claire lay beneath him. "Forever is a long time," he said after several drugging kisses.

She wrapped her arms and legs around him to hold him close. "No it isn't. It's just a notion."

EPILOGUE

A ndor had finished his last Christmas delivery for Nicholas well before dawn. While he couldn't be with a disappointed Claire on Christmas Eve, he had promised nothing would stop him from being with her and Jake on Christmas Day.

He'd returned to her small house in the small hours and found her sound asleep, curled around his pillow. The monitor by her bed emitted shuffling noises, but she didn't awaken. Andor padded to Jake's bedroom and found him sitting up in bed, stopping, rewinding and restarting a favorite section in a Wiggles CD. The TV screen flickered in the otherwise dark room.

Jake's gaze slid briefly to Andor before returning to the TV. "Hi, elf," he said.

Andor grinned and sat down on the bed beside the little boy. In a few hours, Jake's deep Sight, inherited from his mother, would no longer see the accentuated elfin features and pointed ears Andor hid behind his glamour. "Hey Jake, you're up early."

Jake didn't answer, just continued the repeated play of the single scene on his DVD. Andor pulled

Jake's coat and a pair of sandals out of the closet adjacent to the bed. "Come on, Jake. Let's go outside. I have something to show you.

Dressed in Christmas-themed pajamas, socks, sandals and a light coat, his tablet clutched in his hands, Jake followed Andor quietly through the house and out the back door. The sky was still dark, a thin line of gray edging the eastern horizon. Claire's backyard though was ablaze with light.

Tiny fairy sparks shot through the trees, swirling and diving across the lawn before curling around Jake in a luminescent spiral. The boy looked up from his tablet and pointed. The glowing lights bounced off his fingers before flying out into the yard once more. Jake followed, pointing and grasping at the lights by turn, his young features wreathed in a rare smile.

Andor sat down on the patio bench and watched. Firefly season was long past, but it was still dark, and he still possessed his magic for now. He could give Jake fireflies in December.

"That's a fine thing you did. He may never tell you so, but he'll remember this all his days." Nicholas sat down next to Andor. His vestments were travel-stained; there was a crack in his crosier, and sometime during the night he'd lost his mitre. His white hair stood out in all directions, as if he'd been caught in a whirlwind.

Andor looked him up and down. "Did you get in a fight with a jötunn during your deliveries?"

The saint settled back on the bench with a tired sigh, his gaze following Jake who still hunted Andor's fireflies. "No. A djinn."

"Ugh. Nasty piece of work."

"Always."

The two men sat silent for a moment before Andor spoke again. "You're finished early. Don't you have a few million more houses to visit?"

Nicholas spun his cracked crosier in his palms. "Eh, I'm not worried. I'll make it. Besides, this is your last time acting as my overgrown nisse. We should have a few commemorative words, don't you think?"

"'Twas the night before Christmas—"

"Enough. I hate that poem. My stomach doesn't roll like a bowl full of jelly." Nicholas patted his belly. Despite modern popular depictions, Nicholas was a slight, diminutive man. He did sport a luxurious white beard—something to counterbalance his balding pate with its fringe of spiky, windblown hair. What he lacked in stature, he made up for in presence—a blaze of power, magic and wonder all combined into a compassionate heart and soul that shone brighter than any star.

Andor couldn't resist a final dig. "Your dimples are merry."

Nicholas's eyes narrowed. "Son, don't make me close our time together by turning you into a slug."

They both laughed. Nicholas held out his arms. The two men embraced briefly. "Are you sure you want to do this? I can get you to Ljósálfrheimr well before dawn and with plenty of time to deliver my last gifts."

"I'm very sure." Andor had never been so certain of anything in his long existence.

"It's been a good thousand years for me, son. I wasn't too sure at first, but I'm glad Dagrun sent you to me."

Andor rubbed his neck. "And I'm fond of keeping my head attached." The gray line in the east had widened and was now edged in pink. Christmas dawn. The rise of *Solis Invicti.* "You'll still visit? Remember, Claire may no longer believe, but Jake and I do." He turned to the saint and watched, a little saddened, as his mentor's figure began to fade.

Nicholas grinned. "Every year, my boy." He grew more translucent every second, his words softer, fainter. "Look for me beyond the gloaming." Firefly lights danced behind him, lending a halo to his fading image. "When the darkness falls and the moon sails high…"

Andor touched the air where the saint disappeared completely. One firefly light lingered. "And all the stars look down," he replied. "Until next year, my friend."

Lost Letters
And
Christmas Lights

An Elemental Mysteries novella

Elizabeth Hunter

For my family this holiday season:
To those I was born to
And to those I chose
I love you all.
Merry Christmas.

PROLOGUE

Los Angeles, California

"Beatrice?" Giovanni raised his voice only slightly when he entered the house, knowing that despite the massive square footage of the house in San Marino, his mate would be able to hear him.

There was no response.

He pulled off the scarf he'd wrapped around his neck when he'd left the house earlier that evening. The weather in Southern California was mildly cool that December, which meant every native Californian had broken out their warmest wraps. It was so hard following winter fashion when there simply was no winter. Nevertheless, the humans tried.

"Beatrice?" he called again, wondering if she'd left the house. He reached out with his senses.

A hint of chicken *mole* in the air. Caspar had cooked it yesterday.

Doyle, his grey cat, purred near a fire someone had lit in the downstairs sitting room.

No sign of Ben, but that was hardly remarkable this time of night.

He inhaled again.

Vanilla. Acid. Almonds. And a very faint waft of mold.

Giovanni smiled. Beatrice was in the library.

The unmistakable trace of her amnis permeated the air. She'd been in the kitchen recently. Other immortals wouldn't sense it, but Beatrice De Novo wasn't only his wife by human law, she was his vampire mate by tradition. The blood they shared bound them on an elemental level. He always knew when she was near.

Her preternatural senses would have picked up the smallest sound, which meant she was ignoring him. Ignoring him meant one of two things. He calmly walked up the stairs to the second floor, stroking a finger along the side of the Vietnamese vase she'd found for him in Hong Kong the Christmas before.

Beatrice ignoring his call meant she was feeling playful or…

He nudged open the door to the library, leaning against it as he watched her muttering over a table piled with file boxes.

She was in the middle of a project.

"*Ciao bella, Tesoro.*"

She waved one hand, covered in a silk glove because she was handling documents. She didn't lift her head. "Hey. Why are you…" Her mind drifted off before she could finish the question.

"Back so soon?" Giovanni finished for her. "The client wanted the impossible. I refuse to break something out of the National Archives."

"You have before."

"There were multiple copies of that *particular* item." He stepped closer, careful not to touch any of the materials spread over the table. "This item is unique. I'm not interested in depriving a nation of its history—meager though it may be—to satisfy a vampire's whim."

"So kind of you," she muttered, not even rising to the American history taunt. She'd continued her personal research project of documenting daily life in the Mission period of California history that she'd started in graduate school. Giovanni had continued to acquire difficult-to-obtain books and documents for immortal clientele and discreet human collectors. Beatrice helped him when she wanted to, and both kept as busy as they wanted.

It was a good life. Others might think Giovanni longed for the excitement of his nights as an assassin or was jealous of the power others wielded in vampire politics. Power he had handed to them before he stepped away.

But Giovanni Vecchio had no longing for violence. No desire for power. He had spent hundreds of years with both thrust upon him. Now he had found his peace.

He and his mate flew around the world as they liked, visiting their homes and perusing their books. Working when they wanted. Keeping in touch with friends and occasionally assisting with a problem when help was requested.

But for the most part, they lived a quiet life.

"How's the new pub?" She had put down the letter she'd been examining, sliding the acid-free envelope into the file before she pulled out another. "Ben says Gavin's happy as a clam in New York. He's considering making the move permanent. Keeps making noises about the O'Brians, but nothing serious."

"Gavin would gripe about Mother Theresa if he'd spent any time with her. The O'Brians aren't causing him any trouble. And I don't like the manager of Gavin's pub. I miss the one in Houston."

"That's too bad."

"We should go back for a visit."

"To the pub?"

He laughed a little. "To Houston. We could make a visit of it. See Gavin. Charlotte. There's a manuscript exhibit at the Carmichael that I did some work for. I think you'd like it. Looks fascinating."

"Uh-huh."

He sat down and leaned his head in his hand. "We could break into the Rothko Chapel. Finally steal the black canvases you like."

"Yeah...sounds good," she responded, clearly not paying attention. Beatrice was occupied with the letter she held.

It looked like part of the Mission correspondence she'd been collecting.

"What is it?" he asked, giving up on discussing anything other than work.

"Remember the Hungarian you shoved in my direction?"

"The wine collector?"

"Wine*maker*," she corrected. "Rabidly private. Old. I think I may have a lead on that project."

"I thought you'd given up on it."

"No. Put it on the back burner for a bit, but he was getting rude."

Giovanni's head came up. "Explain rude."

Beatrice smiled as he stood and walked to the table. "Nothing I can't handle, handsome. I told him to back off, but then I ran across something when I was helping one of Katya's archivists. There was a mention in a letter from Father Ignacio..."

She trailed off again, but Giovanni started paging through the box of letters, each one a carefully preserved missive from one of the Franciscan priests or secular clergy at California's twenty-one original missions. Over the years, Beatrice had come to know many of the more prolific letter writers by name. Father Ignacio was a favorite.

"He mentions a young priest around San Jose who was an expert in wine-making and had begun sending out '*un informe.*' I think I have some letters that priest exchanged with another in Rome. Odd, I thought at the time, because why Rome? Why not Spain?"

"If he was a member of the clergy, it's possible he—"

"Had connections with someone in the in the church there. I figure that's why. Anyway, I'd misread '*informe*' as a verb, not a noun. But *un informe* would be a…report. An account of some kind. Something written down. At least that's what the context would imply from what I remember."

He paid half a mind to what she was saying and the other half to the excitement in her voice. The animated way her eyes lit up as she tugged the thread of history hidden within the papers before her.

It was almost ridiculous how he loved her.

"So if this priest was writing down his practices and sending them to his contemporaries in the other missions, it might not be just a report, but maybe a journal? A book? Which is exactly what the Hungarian wants and I thought didn't exist. But I think it does! Now I just need to find out how many copies he made of this thing and pray one survived. If I can figure out where he sent them…I'm hoping there's something in the letters to Rome that will give me some more to go on."

Giovanni pursed his lips when he realized what letters she was referring to. "The letters? The… Roman ones? Written from the Vatican?"

"Yes." She closed one box and opened another. "Well, they were written in Rome but were sent to a California Franciscan. So they should be in here. All my Mission correspondence—I just…can't…" She sighed. "This is driving me crazy. I've been looking for hours."

It really was too bad that he hadn't skipped the meeting with the impossible vampire and come home hours ago. "My love, I think I know the letters you're speaking of."

"I know!" Beatrice threw up her hands, and they landed on her hips. "I remember cataloguing them last fall. They should be in this box, but they aren't."

"Well…"

"Gio?" She must have caught the look on his face. "What did you do with my letters?"

"They were written from Rome."

Her eyes narrowed. "Yes, but they were written to a priest in *California.* Clearly, they needed to be with the Mission letters."

"One could argue—" he cleared his throat "—they were more properly filed with Vatican correspondence. Since they were written *from* the Vatican."

Beatrice's mouth dropped open. "You did not."

He shrugged. "You were in the middle of some research with Lucien, and I was having a number of things transferred to the Perugian library, so—"

"Gio, you didn't!" Her hands gripped her hair. "You sent my letters to Fina?"

The library that Giovanni's deceased son had established in Perugia had continued to be run by Serafina Rossi, the human Lorenzo hired to curate the collection in his absence. She truly was a very competent human who had proven to be trustworthy, despite having been chosen by his scheming son. Gradually, Giovanni and Beatrice had enlightened Fina and her son, Enzo, about the immortal world they'd been dragged into unawares. Both had come under Giovanni's protection, and he did not take the responsibility lightly. Plus, Fina was a superb archivist with a background in art history.

"The Perugia library has far more room than this one, Tesoro. And you know I've been transferring materials there when they fit the collection—"

"But they're not Vatican letters! They're Mission letters! I cannot believe you lost my materials—"

He drew up, slightly offended. "I did not 'lose' them. They remain catalogued here, and I put a notation in the files that they were being stored in Perugia with the Vatican papers there."

Slightly mollified, Beatrice stopped yelling, but her angry expression did not wane.

"You took *Mission* letters."

"I took Vatican letters."

"Sent to a mission. *My* mission."

He bit back a laugh. "I do not believe you have a greater claim than the church, my love."

"And I know there's a reference in those letters to this journal or book about wine-making that the Hungarian wants. And it's all the way in Perugia! And I can't ask Fina to dig through all that stuff—"

"There is no 'digging' necessary." He felt his skin heat in anger. "Beatrice, you're acting as if I threw them in a cardboard box and tossed them in a suitcase. I would never—"

"You're right." Her expression softened. "You're right. That was out of line. You would never treat original documents that way."

"Thank you." He was still a bit put out. To think she'd accuse him of being that careless…

"Well," she said. "There's really only one thing to do."

"What?"

Her frown turned to an impish grin. "Clearly, we're spending Christmas in Italy this year."

Christmas in Italy? Away from both of their families and all their employees?

Giovanni tugged Beatrice to him, and her silk-covered hands came up to brush his cheeks as he took her mouth in a lingering kiss.

"What a truly—" he nipped Beatrice's lips and pulled her toward the low couches at one end of the room "—*truly* excellent idea."

"I know." She grabbed his perfectly pressed dress shirt and tore the buttons off as she pulled it open. "I'm brilliant that way."

His fangs dropped as he licked up her neck, murmuring, "*Buon natale* to me."

"Wait!" She pulled away from his kiss. "Is Italy one of those countries that doesn't exchange presents until January?"

"Yes, January 6th. The Epiphany."

"No!"

"You'll survive. Now kiss me."

CHAPTER ONE

Citta di Castello, Perugia
Italy

Serafina Rossi carefully sorted the letters her employers had asked her to find from within the mass of correspondence recently added to the Vecchio Library. Though she understood Dr. Vecchio's reasons, she had to agree with Ms. De Novo's somewhat frantic e-mail. The letters, despite being written from Rome, appeared to belong within De Novo Library in Los Angeles, which specialized in early Californian—particularly Spanish-era—history.

Fina walked around the massive library tables that occupied the floor in the central quadrangle of bookcases. Soft lights illuminated the letters from discreetly hidden sources in the walls of the villa. She reached a long arm to straighten two of the letters, nudging them into a perfect line in chronological order.

Everything was ready for her employers' arrival, and she'd taken a short nap that afternoon in preparation for a late evening, as she always did when Dr. Vecchio or Ms. De Novo was in residence. They stayed in the villa if they needed to use the library for research. She knew they had an estate near Florence, but they preferred to stay in the convenient rooms her former employer had renovated on the second floor.

What they needed the California letters for, she had no idea. But she was a librarian. Her task was to conserve and organize the information, not ask questions.

Written by a young, well-connected Franciscan in Rome, the documents Ms. De Novo had requested were addressed to "my dear friend, Brother Rafael of Mission San Jose" in California. The first were dated in 1798 and the last in 1803. Five years of the earliest correspondence in Mission-era California. They were… not terribly interesting, in Fina's opinion. Speaking mostly of church matters, the earliest were written in a familiar tone. She hadn't had time to read them all yet. The most curious thing was the identity of the writer. "Father P—" was the only designation given.

There were inquiries about the establishment of the mission. A few mentions of holidays, university classes, and mutual acquaintances with very prominent names. These Franciscans were far from country brothers, which made the assignment of the Spanish priest to the California missions rather unusual.

Yes, definitely materials better sorted out in the De Novo Library.

But it was not Fina's job to decide these things. In the two years she'd worked for the Vecchio-De Novo family, she had experienced far more than the usual quirks her colleagues at private libraries reported.

But then, as far as she knew, their employers were entirely human.

"Mama!" Her son, Enzo, called from the front garden. "I think I see the car!"

The winter sun had fallen several hours before, and Enzo was looking forward to their company.

It was a quiet life she and her son lived in Perugia, which did not bother Fina, though the country was beginning to chafe at Enzo, twelve years old and the center of her universe.

Enzo, books, and the odd request from vampire employers. It wasn't the life she thought she'd be living twelve years ago when she finished her time at university, but it had given her independence when her family had shunned her. She was from a small town outside of Venice, and though her parents paid lip service to sophistication, the reality of an unwed daughter expecting a baby made them balk.

Only her grandmother had remained in contact after Enzo was born. And she'd lost her *nonna* when her son was only five.

It was losing Nonna that had hurt the most. Fina had always been a quiet child. It was Nonna who had encouraged her to follow her dreams.

"Fina, dreams will not come to you. You must go out and chase them."

She'd chased them all the way to university, before she'd been swept off her feet and into her professor's bed. His scoffing rejection of her and the baby they'd produced had caused her to retreat.

In her heart, she knew Nonna would be disappointed. But Fina lived for Enzo now. His happiness and security were far more important than her own.

She felt far older than thirty-eight years. She lived alone and didn't fit with the friendly, domestic mothers in the village where her son went to school. Yet rarely could she leave the library that had been her responsibility for twelve years to go to professional conferences or gatherings of her peers. Not only was she a single mother, but the Vecchio Library was her creation. Other than Enzo, its organization was her greatest achievement.

She supposed few would understand that.

Another set of letters caught her eye, tucked into the front pocket of the briefcase on the edge of the table and filed in a manila envelope. Those letters were not written by an eighteenth-century Franciscan but a somewhat mysterious colleague at the Vatican library in Rome.

She'd never met Zeno Ferrara, but the former priest turned immortal had been introduced to her—via handwritten letter, of course—by Dr. Vecchio. In the past two years, Ferrara had offered her a wealth of information regarding anything to do with church history. And though Ferrara was no longer a priest, he still worked at the Vatican Library in some unknown capacity.

They had never met. But through the odd intimacy of their correspondence, Fina had begun to wish that they could.

It was silly, she supposed.

And yet, the often terse letters Ferrara sent had lately shown evidence of…something.

"My dear Signora Rossi, I wonder whether I should be flattered or annoyed by your persistence. Are you always this forward?"

Forward? If she was forward, he was the only one who had ever implied it. The irritating man had put off her question about Pope Alexander VI for over three weeks. When he finally did answer, his letter was so thorough it could have been submitted to an academic journal.

"…I wonder if I should be flattered or annoyed…?"

Flattered? The implication brought a hint of the furious blush to her cheeks that had plagued her since childhood.

"Surely a young woman has better ways of spending a weekend than organizing papal correspondence. Or are the charms of Perugia such that you seek excitement from church relics?"

Well, really.

What kind of man became a priest and then a vampire, anyway? Did he look like the priests she'd grown up with, paternal men with cheerful faces and kind eyes? Or would he look like the vampires she'd met when Dr. Vecchio or Ms. De Novo had brought visitors? Beautiful—almost all the vampires she'd met were beautiful—but remote. Cold. Her employers seemed to be exceptions to the rule. From the wry humor that slipped through Signore Ferrara's letters, she thought Signore Ferrara might be, too. Their letters had begun professionally but became familiar. Past his quips, Fina could see that Zeno Ferrara had a passion for his work that she could appreciate.

What would he look like?

She couldn't imagine. And, she supposed, it was better that she didn't. Ferrara was a colleague. It behooved her to remain aloof should they ever meet. Daydreaming about what the vampire's eyes might look like was a childish distraction.

She heard the car doors slam shut, then Enzo began shouting in rapid Italian despite the English she'd so carefully tutored him in.

"Dr. Vecchio, this car is—"

"Please, Enzo." A laughing voice interrupted her son. "You must call me Giovanni. How many times have I asked now?"

"My mother would not want me to be so informal, Signore."

"*Signore* Giovanni, then," a woman's voice suggested. "And Signora Beatrice for me."

"If you like," Enzo said politely just as Fina reached the door.

"Dottore, Signora," she said, holding out a hand as their driver stowed the car and himself...somewhere. There was always a near-invisible human servant or driver escorting the Vecchio-De Novos everywhere they went. They didn't carry phones or briefcases; the driver did. Fina had almost become accustomed to it. "Welcome," she said. "It is so good to see you."

"Please, Fina," Beatrice pled with her. "Please call me Beatrice. There is no need to be so formal."

Fina hesitated. She'd allowed herself to become familiar with her former employer—going so far as to consider Paulo a friend—only to discover after he had died that he was not a good man at all, but rather a vicious monster who had killed many, including Beatrice's own father. Only for Serafina and Enzo had he redeemed himself. Paulo—*Lorenzo*—had reserved all of his humanity for them.

She didn't know why. She would never understand. But she had learned caution. Things were not always what they appeared to be in the vampire world.

But if her employers wished her to be more familiar, she would be.

"Of course," she said with a smile. "Beatrice. Giovanni. How are you both?"

"Well, thank you," Giovanni replied. "As always, we appreciate your accommodating us."

"Of course. Signora Giannini has prepared the upstairs rooms for you if you'll be staying here."

"We will be," Beatrice said. "Thanks, Fina." Beatrice's eyes lit up. "Now, let's see those letters."

Fina saw Enzo's face fall, just a little. He masked it quickly.

But not too quickly for Giovanni to have caught it.

"I'd love to stretch my legs a bit," he said, kissing Beatrice with easy affection. "Why don't you and Fina start and maybe I could trouble Enzo to kick a ball with me for a bit."

"Yes, of course," the boy exclaimed. "Let me go to the house."

Fina glanced down at Doctor Vecchio's impeccably polished shoes.

"Dottore—"

"Again," he interrupted. "Please, call me Giovanni. And I am happy to play a bit of football with your son if he is willing to indulge me." He winked at her. "My nephew is too busy for me these days. And Enzo is a good boy."

Fina's heart melted. "Of course. He is very excited to have you both visit."

Beatrice smiled. "We've been looking forward to seeing him, too." She hooked Fina's arm with hers. "Now, let's leave the boys to their games and go look at my letters."

"She's so lonely," Beatrice said later that night, after she and Giovanni had locked themselves in the secure, lightproof room on the second floor of the library. Rudy, the young valet Caspar was training, had taken the small room off the garage.

"Who?" He frowned, looking up from the book he'd been reading. "Serafina?"

"Mmhmm." Beatrice pulled her earrings off and set them on the dresser in the lavish suite Lorenzo had designed. They hadn't had time to redecorate it, but it wasn't as ostentatious as most of Giovanni's late son's holdings. "I think she works too much. This library is her life."

Giovanni frowned, as if he didn't quite understand why that was a problem.

Her husband. Five hundred years old, and still somewhat clueless about the female of the species.

"So what is it that you want to do?" he asked. "Move the library? We cannot do that. I mean, we could, but it would be horribly wasteful. Lorenzo may have been a monster, but this facility…"

It was the one thing that his son had ever done right. Possibly the only humanity Lorenzo had retained. And she knew it was one of the reasons Giovanni liked to be here. Maybe why he hadn't changed a thing. Not even their room.

"I don't want to move the library," she said. "The library is perfect." The slight tension in his shoulders disappeared. "And I think Fina likes to be here. She's a quiet person. But maybe we should make an effort to see that she leaves occasionally. Think about it, Gio."

"She's isolated here." He nodded. "Yes, I can see that."

"She's estranged from her family. She and her son occupy that weird between place of living in both the vampire world and the human one. It's not like she's in LA where Enzo could go to Ben's school and be around other day people's children. Who does she confide in? Where does she vent?"

Giovanni said, "I hadn't thought of that. But you're correct. If I think about our human employees at home, they mostly socialize with us or other vampire employees. There is a community there. Here, there is none."

"Matt and Dez. My grandma and Caspar. Rudy has already become friendly with everyone. Fina has no one here. If she were closer to Rome…" Beatrice shrugged.

"It's not even three hours by car. She could visit there if she liked. Even use the house in town. Angela would love it."

Beatrice smiled. "We need to offer it to her. She would never ask. She's still so formal with us."

It bothered Beatrice. Unlike many immortals, who chose not to grow attached to their mortal helpers, she considered most of their employees family. Granted, she was young. She knew it would be harder to bear the loss over hundreds, possibly thousands, of years. But Giovanni treated them the same, and he was far older than her.

Beatrice stripped, the feeling of cool air against her sensitive skin welcome after the stifling confinement of winter clothes. She now understood why her husband preferred to be naked. Any clothing was uncomfortable, though it was a discomfort she had learned to live with. She shuddered to think about the poor immortals who had lived through more restrictive fashion periods of history. Corsets? No, thank you.

But one had to blend. It kept the rest of the world comfortable. Beatrice still felt, in many ways, very human. Though there were differences between them, her best friend and assistant, Dez, was still her closest confidante. And though she'd once been a loner, she had created close relationships with her vampire family and her friends.

But still, Fina kept her distance. No doubt, the revelations about Lorenzo had shaken her. But the woman was still there. She could have run away, but she'd stayed. Probably for the books.

Glancing at her husband, whose nose was back buried in his novel, she decided it was definitely for the books.

"You know what?" Beatrice mused. "She's kind of…you. A human female version of you."

"What?" He looked up, frowning. "Who's me?"

She smiled as she sauntered over to the bed. Dawn was still an hour or so away, so her mate would have plenty of energy. And Beatrice decided that he definitely needed distracting. She crawled up the bed and took the book from his hands, setting it on the side table.

"Mmm," he murmured. "Hello, my wife."

She straddled his legs and brushed the hair off his forehead. He'd been wearing his dark brown curls long again.

"Oh yeah," she said, leaning down to bite the edge of his ear. "You're definitely pulling off the sexy, yet distracted, professor thing."

"I am not distracted anymore."

He put both hands on her hips, teasing the lace of her panties where they lay on her skin. Now that sensation, she enjoyed.

"I was saying that Serafina is a female, human version of you, Professor."

"Hmm." His fangs fell, and he traced them lightly over the skin on her neck. "That's 'Dottore' to you. And let us conference on this particular topic at another time, Signorina. I don't find it pertinent to the topic at hand." His hand stroked down and cupped her under her panties.

"Oh, Dottore Vecchio," she whispered. "I'm not sure we should be having this conversation. It seems so unprofessional."

"It's highly unprofessional," he said. Giovanni swiftly rolled them over so she was under him, and within seconds, the delicate lace panties were scraps on the floor.

Then, Beatrice's husband proceeded to ace every single sexy-professor fantasy she'd ever had. With honors.

"You're incredibly detail oriented," she panted hours later. "Yay for me."

His cheeks were flushed with the blood he'd taken from the inside of her thigh. "I pride myself on being thorough."

"Well done."

He grabbed her chin and covered her mouth in a hard kiss, which slowly turned soft as he settled next to her in bed. She could feel the dawn coming in her blood. Giovanni still slept during the day, and on mornings when she'd taken his blood, she could sleep a little herself. Her own special version of afterglow.

"You know," he said, his eyes closing. "If you think Serafina is a female version of me, then all she really needs to be happy is her own version of you, Tesoro."

Beatrice smiled and slid over to rest next to him, her body relaxed but her mind humming.

Another version of herself? Thinking of the letters she'd spotted peeking out of Fina's briefcase, an idea began to form.

It was Christmas in Italy. Perhaps Beatrice could work a little magic of her own.

"You want Enzo and me to join you in Rome?" Fina looked between Giovanni and Beatrice with wide eyes. "For Christmas? I am very flattered to be asked, but—"

"Don't feel flattered, Fina, feel welcome," Beatrice urged her. "Please join us. We don't know many people in the city, and we'd love to have you and Enzo join us. Surely you won't be working while he's on holiday from school."

"Well no, but—"

Giovanni said, "Holidays are always so much more enjoyable with children around."

"Even though you heathens don't exchange presents until January," Beatrice muttered.

He turned to her. "Again? We're having this argument again?"

"Epiphany. I have to wait until January to get presents. So unfair."

"Such an American," Giovanni said before he turned back to Fina. "My housekeeper in Rome is beside herself that we came without Ben, though he is hardly a child any longer. Angela would be delighted to have both of you come with us."

Could she? Most Christmases with Enzo were quiet affairs. She would build a small *ceppo* and fill it with lights and small gifts, always letting Enzo put the star on the top. She hung gold lights in the house and baked the *panatone* her grandmother had taught her.

"Sweet bread for a sweet year, my Serafina."

Gifts were often small when Enzo was young and she didn't have much money to spare, but the little presents always appeared like magic to his child's eyes. Christmas was quiet. Simple. She liked it that way.

"Per favore, Mama! Please, please, can we go to Rome? I want to hear the pipes and flutes and there are all the trees. Please, Mama! I can tell all my friends—"

"Enzo, we do not boast of generosity," she whispered to her son. "Dottore Vecchio and—"

"Beatrice and *Giovanni,"* her employer said, smiling, "would be very happy if you joined them." Then Giovanni nudged Enzo's shoulder and said, "And you should definitely hear the *zampognari* and *pifferai.* Though I warn you, some are quite bad." He laughed. "We'll find some good ones for you."

"Please, Fina," Beatrice said. "We're staying until the Epiphany and we'd love it if you would join us." She paused. "And while I know you won't officially be working, there is a possibility that I'll be able to search the Vatican Library for more information regarding the Mission letters. I'd love to have your help."

Fina tried to stop the color she could feel rising in her cheeks. "The Vatican library?" Where Zeno Ferrara worked?

Surely, Beatrice didn't intend...

"I wrote to my friend Zeno before we came," Beatrice said. "And I think he might have an idea who the priest in Rome was. I'm sure we'd be allowed to visit the library."

Giovanni frowned. "You wrote to Zeno?"

"Of course," Beatrice said. "Didn't I tell you?"

They exchanged a look that Fina couldn't interpret because her mind was racing.

Beatrice continued. "You two have exchanged letters, haven't you? About some of the collection here?"

"Yes," she said. "I...Yes, Signore Ferrara and I have corresponded. He's been very helpful."

"Excellent! I'm sure he'd enjoy meeting a colleague with so many of the same interests. Zeno is passionate about preservation."

There went her stomach. This was ridiculous. She was not a schoolgirl. "Passionate?"

"Oh yes," Giovanni said, smiling at his wife. "Zeno is a man of very strong passions. About books and...history. And terrorizing his assistants."

"Ignore him," Beatrice said. "Zeno's lovely. He worked in the Italian resistance during World War II, did you know that? When he was still a priest. I believe he's from Naples originally. I think he was quite the problem child within the church."

"That's fascinating."

Rome for Christmas? Taking Enzo to see the lights and music of the great city. Sharing lodging and meals—best not to think about that one—with her employers, who were quite obviously trying to make her a friend.

Seeing the Vatican Library.

Possibly meeting the man—the vampire—who'd been the subject of so many flights of imagination.

'A man of very strong passions,' Giovanni had said.

Oh, Nonna, she thought. *You didn't teach me anything about this.*

What would her Nonna say? A quiet family Christmas with her son or the mysteries of the Vatican library and a holiday with vampires?

She knew exactly what Nonna would say.

"Pack your red underthings. Red is good luck."

"I'll go," Fina said, watching Enzo erupt with joy. "We'll go. Thank you for the invitation."

CHAPTER TWO

Vatican City, Italy

Z eno Ferrara erupted from the table. "You are an idiot. A brainless, directionless idiot! Has the collar cut off all the circulation to your head?"

The young priest paled and stepped back. "But Brother Zeno—"

"And I am not your brother anymore!" He raked his hands through the hair that hung in his eyes. He needed a haircut. Again. But if these stupid young priests didn't stop misfiling his documents, he was never going to leave the archives.

The young human took another step back.

"Are you going to bite me?" he whispered.

Zeno's head turned to the vaulted ceiling of his workroom. "Father God," he shouted, "save me from imbeciles before it comes to murder."

He heard the footsteps behind him and spun in a blur.

"Please stop scaring the young ones, Zeno." Arturo Leon raised a lazy eyebrow as he entered the room. "It's getting harder and harder to find you assistants."

That prompted a flurry of arguments in Latin between the two men. Old arguments they'd had for decades, with a few new digs thrown in. Zeno barely noticed when the young priest who'd lost the box of eighteenth-century correspondence slipped out of the room.

"I never thought I'd say this, my friend, but I believe you need a holiday." Arturo sat down at the table and crossed his legs, examining the odd assortment of papers, inks, quills, pens, magnifying loupes, and different artificial lights that decorated the center of the table. Zeno zipped around the rows of bookshelves, looking for the box he'd set out the night before. The box that had been misfiled somewhere within the cavernous room Zeno considered his own.

He finally stopped the blur of movement, appearing before the old priest with a grey document box in his hands. A box that looked exactly like the thousands of others that filled the room. A single string of numbers on the front was the only identifier.

"It may be in here." Zeno set it down on the table. "And I don't have time for a holiday."

"You do realize how odd that sounds coming from someone who is immortal."

"Yes, yes. But Vecchio and Beatrice will be here in an hour. And while three hours would have been more than enough time for me to go through the letters from California and find the ones they are looking for, now I cannot even find the box. Because of idiots with more devotion than brains!"

"Careful, Zeno. And why are we allowing Vecchio into the archives? He's a known thief."

"That all depends on how you define thief. He's a scholar. A respected one. His other skills are secondary, and it's not like you haven't used them in the past."

Arturo sniffed. "I don't know what you're talking about."

Zeno grinned. "Liar. Only one man could have procured that very elusive—and inconvenient—gospel from Ethiopia. How many copies were there?"

"Only two."

"And now both are tucked away in your secret rooms, Arturo. And Vecchio is granted access to mine. I don't expect any objections."

"You presume much, Ferrara."

Zeno ignored Arturo, who'd been no more than a baby when Zeno had been turned in 1938. Now, the child had become an old man, a powerful one. In charge of all immortal clergy and laypeople attached to the Catholic Church, Arturo wasn't a bad sort of human. In fact, Zeno considered him more of a friend than any others of the stuffed Church bureaucracy. The fact that he had to wade through their politics still chafed, even though he'd been doing it for over sixty years.

But he had more freedom and resources here than anywhere else, and the documents, the *letters*, were his calling.

They filled the cavernous room, missives from all over the world, stretching back as long as humans had taken pen to paper or parchment to communicate with others at a distance. He found the letters, procured any with even a passing link to the church, and then he dissected them. The authors, the recipients. Where and when were they written? Who did they mention? Correspondence was his passion.

The modern blasphemy of e-mail, his bane.

Mostly, Zeno was left alone, which suited him. He's been released from his earthly vows ten years after he'd been made immortal, as he'd felt unable to serve the church and remain steadfast in immortality. It was one thing for a human to reform at age thirty-five and take vows to God for the next forty years. Quite another to face an eternity of sacrifice with no end in sight. Zeno decided he could serve God far better if he retained his sanity. And his humor.

Maybe the young priests didn't see his humor, but it was there.

Sometimes.

The bits of socializing he did were with others of his kind. His life was his work. History was written by the victors, but the letters…letters told the true tale. Zeno Ferrara specialized in the discovery of secrets hidden within the handwritten word.

He glanced at the letter from Beatrice De Novo, whom he'd met only two years before. He'd known her mate far longer and was enormously pleased that his old friend had found a wife who was so like-minded. Beatrice was a delight, though he'd never cease arguing with her about the sacrilege of electronic communication.

Thank God computers had no place in his library.

The letters. Again. His eyes stole back to them. Letters were truth. Not only the words written but how they were written. What pace did the pen keep upon the page? Where did the writer hesitate? Where did she rush? Sometimes, he could fancy the pen in his own hand, the letters stretching out across his skin.

Giovanni and I will be in Rome over Christmas, and I'm really hoping you'll have some insight to this set of documents. If you have any of the complementary letters or know anything about the writer, we'd be so grateful, Zeno. We'll be in Perugia before we travel to Rome.

Perugia. Vecchio had an enormous private library in Citta di Castello, though he'd never visited. The librarian there…

Serafina Rossi.

He could see her name written neatly across the bottom of the very professional letters she'd written to Zeno about one matter or another. He always enjoyed answering them because the woman asked excellent questions and after some correspondence, her letters contained a prim wit that intrigued him. The handwriting told him she was young and educated. But it told him nothing of her hair. Or her eyes.

Which were really none of his business, were they?

Except he wanted to know. More than one of his acquaintances had mentioned the "unique charms of the Vecchio Library," and he doubted they were talking about the bookcases or the stained glass.

What did she look like as she wrote to him? Did she have long hair, tied back as she worked? Was it short, mussed from hands tugging it in concentration? Did she wear glasses?

He had a weakness for women in glasses.

Did she curl over her desk as she wrote her very proper responses to him or sit upright with shoulders held carefully?

Did her lips purse when she wrote his name?

Her signature vexed him. The neatness of her given name was misleading. It was the sensual dip and swell when she signed *Rossi* that had caught Zeno's attention.

Fina.

Beatrice had once referred to the librarian as "Fina" in a letter.

Fina. Shortened form of Serafina, a name drawn from the Biblical "seraphim." Hebrew in origin. It meant "the burning ones."

A fiery name signed with such control.

Fina.

What would it look like in her own hand? Would the *F*'s angled upstroke be pointed like a dagger? Would the downstroke dip and swell beneath the line?

Zeno felt his lips curve into a smile. Over their two years of correspondence, he had to admit he'd developed a bit of a preoccupation with the woman. She understood passion for work as he did. He would be most intrigued to see Fina sign her first name.

Perhaps she would accompany Vecchio and Beatrice.

But probably not. Beatrice had mentioned a child who lived on the property, and it was doubtful that a young woman with a family would want to be away during the Christmas holiday. There were things to celebrate. Gifts to exchange.

Rubbing the silver-dotted stubble he'd let grow for months, Zeno tried to remember the last time he'd celebrated Christmas. The 1980s? Surely it hadn't been that long. But then, he rarely took holidays. The few bits of leisure time he indulged in were spent with the two other immortals in Vatican City, playing the hardest, fastest football the three could manage without tearing up the carefully manicured lawns. Both the other vampires were priests and needed the physical challenge as much as he did. He really ought to take up mountain climbing again, but that would take too much time away from work.

Nobody understood the work.

He dove back into the box of letters, smiling when he found the one he'd been hunting.

Mission San Jose, 1798

My dear Pietro, you cannot imagine this land we have found...

"You're here."

Giovanni looked up from his notebook to see his old friend, but the vampire was looking past him. He glanced over his shoulder to see Beatrice and Fina following him down the hall. He muffled the smile. It seemed that Beatrice had not been far off in her suspicions. Clever woman.

"Ferrara." Giovanni held out his hand, startling the man back to awareness. "So good to see you again. What has it been? Seven years or so?"

Zeno frowned. "What are you talking about? I received a letter from you in April."

"Of course." He held out a hand for Beatrice's. "I know you met my lovely wife last year."

"Zeno," Beatrice said. "So good to see you again. I cannot thank you enough for your help with this. Between the four of us, I just know we're going to track down this manuscript."

"The four of us," Zeno repeated.

Was Giovanni the only one who noticed the man's eyes darting to Fina repeatedly? He doubted it, as the woman's face had taken on more than a bit of color.

"Yes," Beatrice said. "I know you've corresponded, but Zeno, let me introduce Fina to you. Serafina Rossi, our librarian in Perugia. Fina, this is Zeno Ferrara, former priest, handwriting expert, and terror of the Vatican."

"Hello." Zeno held out his hand and folded both of them around Fina's palm when they touched. "Ignore her. She married a fire vampire, so she's clearly not sane. It is such a pleasure to finally meet you, Signora Rossi."

"*Signorina* Rossi," Fina answered quietly. "Please, call me Fina. And it is a pleasure to meet you, as well, Signore Ferrara." She looked around the room with a slight smile. "The scope of your work…You have understated it in your letters. It is monumental. Detailed handwriting and historical analysis on so many documents. I cannot imagine such a project. Truly a work for the ages."

"Please, you must call me Zeno." He couldn't keep his eyes off her. "I have been so impressed with the reports I have heard from Perugia. I understand the collection was completely unorganized when you arrived."

Beatrice couldn't stop the smile no matter how much she bit her lip.

The two librarians wandered toward the worktable, chattering like old friends, and Giovanni sidled up to his wife.

"Do you see it?" she asked almost silently, well aware of Zeno's sharp hearing. No matter, the vampire's gaze was locked on Fina's, rapt on every word that left her mouth.

"I see it."

"They're *perfect* for each other. I forgot how handsome Zeno is. Nothing like you, but he definitely has the rumpled-professor-sexy going on."

"Is that supposed to be flattering?" He tried not to laugh at her. "It's certainly a face that drew much attention before he joined the church."

She gasped a little. "Zeno's a reformed scoundrel? Exactly what Fina needs! How did I miss this?

"Perhaps because it is none of your business."

"Pfft." She punched him playfully in the stomach. "Whatever. I've got an eternity for whatever business needs doing. This is going to be great."

He stopped and put a hand on the small of her back. "She's human, Tesoro."

"So was I."

Her eyes told him she knew exactly what he was saying.

"There are no guarantees of happily ever after here," Giovanni said.

She smiled a little ruefully. "That's life, isn't it? No guarantees about anything. We make the best of what we have. Every day. And I have a feeling both those two have been putting off really *living* for too long."

How could he not kiss her?

"Meddler," he whispered as their lips parted.

"I know." She swiftly kissed the corner of his mouth. "Since I don't have any presents—"

"You're getting presents! You just get them in January."

"I have to amuse myself somehow."

"I'm glad you're amused."

"Gio, what would you have done if I hadn't wanted to turn?"

His smile fell. "Come. We should get started. I can hear the priests' nervous pacing at the thief among their books."

Two hours later, they had found all the letters from the young priest in California that Zeno suspected he had in the collection. There might have been more, but there was no way of knowing. Between him and Beatrice, they'd checked every box of unexamined correspondence from the New World and found three more letters, on top of the seven he'd found before. Combined with the letters from the Roman priest, they constituted a total of twenty-five documents.

They began sorting by date, the letters from Brother Rafael in California on one side, the ones from Brother Pietro in Rome on another.

Zeno tried to focus on the letters and not the distracting Fina Rossi.

When she walked in, he'd known it was her. Zeno didn't know why or how, he just knew. It wasn't her thick hair the color of chestnuts or the deep brown eyes, for he hadn't known she possessed those. Or a set of sensuously full lips. Or a rather stunning figure.

Perhaps it was the look of quiet excitement on her face. Serafina of the intriguing letters would be quietly excited to visit the famed Vatican Library. Perhaps it was the very professional black briefcase she carried with a hint of whimsy in the red striped lining that peeked from an open pocket.

Perhaps he simply knew. From her blood. The pulse of which heightened the moment their eyes met. From her scent, which was touched with vanilla and almonds. As if the scent of crumbling paper perfumed her skin.

Zeno wanted to write his name across that skin. Trail the ink over the soft white of her arm and lose his stained fingers in the fall of her hair.

His reaction knocked him sideways. Zeno had not wanted a woman like that in a long, long time.

"What is this manuscript you mentioned, Beatrice?" He had to stop fantasizing about Fina's skin. This wasn't the time.

"*Mnrf.*" Beatrice took the pencil from her mouth. "I have a client looking for a manuscript detailing wine-cultivation practices in California during the mission period. He's eccentric. He told me that a priest working at one of the missions had written it, but he had no idea who the priest was or where this manuscript might have gone. I'd put it off for a while until I found a clue in another of the letters in my collection."

"The ones that Gio sent to Fina?" He raised his head and winked at the woman, only to see she'd put on reading glasses to look closer.

Her lips were pursed. Her hair twisted up in a knot secured with a pencil.

Dear God...

She smiled. "I believe this was in another set of letters. Giovanni had already sent me the ones here because they were written by a Roman priest and he thought they belonged with the Vatican correspondence in the Vecchio Library in Perugia."

"I've heard what an impressive collection it is."

Her eyes lit talking about her work. It was... entrancing.

"It is so diverse," she said. "At first, I could make nothing of the theme, but over time, I began to see that all the documents—save for a few pieces here and there—related to the virtue and progress of humanity. It is a primer, so to speak, of the ideal Classical individual. A map of self-improvement, if you will, gathered through the greatest periods of human achievement."

He saw Giovanni grimace and suspected some of the rumors he'd heard about the fire vampire's sire must be correct.

"A fascinating collection, then. I hope to see it someday."

There was the rush of her blood again. He didn't think she feared him, so it must be pleasure? Excitement to share her work?

"Of course, Signore Ferrara—"

"Zeno."

"Zeno." Her pulse didn't slow. "We often have visiting scholars. You would be most welcome."

How many of those scholars came to examine the books, and how many to see the beautiful, demure director of the Vecchio Library? How many were vampires like himself? He felt his fangs drop on instinct, so he looked back at the table, not wanting her to notice.

She had turned back to her own work by the time he wrestled his instincts under control.

He did not become possessive of humans. It was not his priority, and he had chosen not to indulge that aspect of his immortal nature. His assignations with women over the years had been friendly but casual. Respectful, always. For the offer of blood, the giving of it, was as sacred to him now as it had ever been. In war. In the sacrament. Blood was life..

But Zeno would be the worst sort of liar if he didn't confess that he wanted Fina's.

Though young vampires such as him could be highly possessive, he'd always fought against it. He had given up all possessions when he joined the church. Given up the wealth gained through lying and manipulation. And though he drew a generous salary for his work at the Vatican, he lived simply.

He had learned as a human: Earthly possessions had a way of owning their master.

And to possess one such as her? Infinitely more dangerous.

"I think I have something," she said, flipping the paper over. "It is in the postscripts on back. I had overlooked them because they don't refer to anything related to wine. But if we're looking for the identity of the writer, I think they might be compelling. I believe these two priests were quite close, as it appears the Roman priest—"

"Brother Pietro."

"Yes, Pietro—might have been counseling Rafael in some spiritual matter."

Zeno said, "I've just sorted these and I'm beginning to skim the contents. I believe you're correct. Look at 1801."

Zeno and Fina moved down the table, standing across from each other as they looked for the correct letter and its response.

"Here," she said. "In May. This is what I saw. In the second to last paragraph, it reads: 'I urge you, brother, to fight against this temptation. For you know there can be no end that will satisfy God or yourself. Pray for guidance and confess to your brothers there. But do not...do not be tempted.' Please forgive my Spanish; it is not the best." She stopped and looked at Zeno. "What was in the letter before this one? To what is he referring?"

Zeno found the one dated before the letter Fina had read. He skimmed it, but there was nothing. Nothing but the day-to-day life of the mission. The concern about a sudden disease that had struck the animals. He flipped it over to examine the back of the letter. Eight small words sat lonely on the back of the page.

I cannot stop my thoughts turning to Antonia.

"Antonia," he said. "He cannot stop thinking of *Antonia.* Was Father Rafael in love?"

Beatrice moved next to him, taking the letter from his hands. "Who was she?"

Giovanni asked, "Is there any way of knowing? She could have been anyone."

Fina said, "She was obviously known to both of them. A relative of Pietro's perhaps?"

Beatrice asked, "What kind of records does the church keep on eighteenth-century Franciscans? Anything?"

"Hmm." Zeno thought he might know of someone who would know, but the human would be sleeping at two in the morning. "Let me work on that tomorrow. For now, let's see what else we can find."

Beatrice frowned. "Not that I don't love a good mystery, but does this have anything to do with a manuscript on early viticulture?"

"You want to know where your book went, no?" Zeno growled. "It seems to me that the more we find out about Brother Rafael, the more we might be able to trace his manuscript. Fina, do you have the next?"

"The next after the mention of Antonia is the one I read before," she said. "It would be Rafael's turn to respond."

He looked up; her heart was racing again.

"Are you all right, *cara*?"

"Fine." She flushed. "Thank you."

"Are you tired? I forget that you are not a monster of the night like me."

That got a smile out of her. "I'd hardly call you monstrous."

"Wait till you see me in a temper."

A crooked smile curved her lips. "I cannot imagine."

Giovanni burst into laughter, and Zeno threw a sharpened pencil at his face, which he caught easily.

"The next letter, Zeno. Before I tell her all your secrets."

"Very well." He walked down the line. "Ah, here. 'My dear brother, only you know how much I honor her. Only you know how pure our love. How can such be called a sin? For I carry her in my heart in this foreign place. She is light.'" He glanced up, feeling Fina's eyes on him. "'Though I know she cannot be mine, still I long for her happiness.'"

Wordlessly, Fina picked up the next letter and scanned it.

"Here, just at the bottom: 'Though your sincerity is honorable, yet our faith must bid you to abandon this, brother. For other purposes mark your steps. Purposes far greater than earthly temptations.'"

Zeno found the next letter.

"'Do the scriptures not write that God himself is love? Brother, I cannot abandon hope when I have no word that hope is lost. For the lady's devotion remains true, though I am oceans away from her. I go to Santa Maria tomorrow. I must pray.'"

Fina read again, already finding the next letter Father Pietro had written.

"'My dear brother, surely you must see that there is no hope. For our vows are eternal—'"

Zeno broke in. "Obviously, that's not true."

Fina smiled and continued, "'—and our work is God's own. What comparison is there between... fleshly gratification and heavenly delight?'"

Zeno cocked his head. "I'm rather sure there can be both. Very well, here's the next from our boy, Rafael. Don't buy it, brother," he muttered to the page. "'He writes, 'And yet, my dear Pietro, my devotion is steadfast. Had all hope been lost for me, I know you would have written of it. Therefore, I shall hope. And though an ocean separate us, and the world condemn us, I believe heaven does not.'"

Beatrice crossed over to read over Zeno's shoulder. "That's beautiful."

Fina read, "'I cannot deceive you that the lady remains unattached, though faithful to her family and to God. Her position in society is uncertain should she remain unwed. And what have you, a poor Franciscan, to offer her, even were you to abandon your vows? I plead with you to flee from this strange attachment.'"

"A harsh fate," Giovanni said. "Even if Rafael had abandoned his vows, he stood to return to his lady with nothing. Would he even be able to return to Spain? Was Antonia Spanish or Italian? It seems clear that though Rafael was of the Spanish church, Pietro was a Roman."

Beatrice picked up the next letter and handed it to Zeno.

"Only one line at the bottom of the page: 'My soul is in agony. Surely God must save me from this.'"

"'Pray, my brother,'" Fina read back to him, her voice aching. "'For God does not desire his children suffer pain such as this. Pray and devote yourself to your work.'"

"'I cannot pray,'" Zeno read from the next, his own heart beating once as he listened to her. "'For what are empty words against this despair? Without her, the light is gone. My work brings me no joy without the contemplation of her countenance. I see her smile within the sun. Her hair in the trailing vines I tend. I can only touch them since I cannot reach her.'"

"'I beg of you, brother—'" there were tears at the corner of Fina's eyes "'—to tend your vines as you would tend the one you love. What purpose is there in this world without the Lord's mission? I mourn for your pain. Devote yourself to God's work as you would devote yourself to her. For in this, you must find the satisfaction lost to you in this life. And know that this world is only a prelude to the next. There is still hope.'"

Was there still hope?

Zeno skimmed through the last letter. He read it. Read it again, the words locked in his mind. Then he let his eyes meet Fina's as he recited Rafael's last missive.

"'I will come for her. I have no choice. She is all that is light and beauty in my life. My soul is but a mirror of her own. My heart, her twin in devotion. Surely God cannot condemn us. Surely the world must be kind. I will come for her, though oceans separate us. I have a plan. Tell my love to wait for me. I beg you, my brother, tell her I shall come. For what is an ocean against eternity?'"

Zeno let his eyes fall back to the page. "Presidio de Monterey, 1803."

CHAPTER THREE

Rome, Italy

*F*or what is an ocean against eternity?

He was so much more than she had imagined. Fina lay in her bed, breathless at the memory of Zeno's voice, reading the letters as if the two of them had *been* the lovers, parted by fate.

The dark tangle of his hair, touched with silver at the temples. The laugh lines at the corner of his eyes. He must have been in his forties when he'd been turned. Unusual, from what she had learned. But then what did she know? She was a child in his world, stumbling through life with her organizer and briefcase, assisting those far wiser than herself.

He seemed so very human…until he did not. She could see the flashes of predatory awareness in him when his temper slipped. The body that moved just a little too fast. She did suspect, as Beatrice had called him, that he could be the "terror of the Vatican." For surely a man—a vampire—like Zeno was no tame thing.

How did he feel so familiar? Was it his letters, which had so perfectly captured Zeno's mercurial personality and gruff humor? It had to be. Fina had felt immediately comfortable despite having never met him before. This stranger. This vampire! It was if their minds were already familiar, even if their bodies were not.

The way he'd watched her…Even miles away from Vatican City, in the luxurious Vecchio home, she could still feel his eyes.

"Mama?"

She heard Enzo's sleepy voice from the hall. They'd only returned an hour before dawn. Fina was both exhausted and wired by the night. She lay in her bed, dressed for sleep, but sleep did not find her.

"Come in, Enzo."

Her boy pushed open the door. Twelve years old. Where had the years gone? Soon he would be a man. Her heart ached a little at the knowledge, even as she felt a surge of pride. She had done this. No one had helped her, save for Giovanni's son. She had raised Enzo. Loved him. Taught him. And she had done well.

Enzo rolled onto the side of the bed, rubbing sleepy eyes. "Did you just get home? How was the library?"

"It was fascinating, darling, but why are you awake?"

"I heard you come in, I think. The gate…"

"Ah, of course." The gate to the massive old house was very close to his room. "I'll be sure to be quieter tonight. We were talking loudly, I think."

He nodded, his eyes falling closed. "I should go back to bed."

"Yes, do. I'll be sleeping late today, I think. Do you have plans?"

"Angela said something about the market." He yawned and sat up. "And Rudy and I are helping her decorate the house. She's fun."

"Such a good boy." She ruffled his hair. "What would I do without you?"

"Get lots of work done, and be very boring."

"Oh." She groaned and rolled into the pillow as he laughed. "You know your mama."

"Did you have fun?" he asked. "You sounded like you had fun at the library."

"I did," she said. "It's a wonderful thing to love your work."

"Good." He leaned down and kissed her cheek. "Good night. Good day, I mean." He bared his teeth. "Soon you'll be just like the vampires."

She laughed, but within minutes of Enzo closing the door, Fina had fallen asleep.

When she woke, it was to the dip of her bed. Fina opened her eyes to see Beatrice leaning over, fangs hanging down in her smiling mouth.

"*Aah!*" Fina sat bolt upright, scrambling toward the headboard.

"Hey!" Beatrice said. "Sorry I surprised you, but you will not believe what I found out today!"

"Are you going to bite me?"

Finally understanding that Fina was terrified, Beatrice leaned back. "What? No."

"But your—" Fina motioned to her mouth, heart pounding. "They're just...long and—and sharp. And you're not going to bite me?"

Beatrice cocked her head. "Do you want me to bite you?"

"No!"

"This—" she waved at her mouth "—happens for a lot of reasons. Excitement is one of them. Sorry, I was just so jazzed about what I found. I'll have to keep that in mind." She smiled, and Fina noticed her fangs were a little shorter. "Sorry."

"It's okay." It really wasn't, but Fina did understand her employers were not human. She knew that. Maybe she just didn't know that as well as she thought.

Fangs. Long, sharp fangs.

Zeno would have them too.

"You were the last one sleeping," Beatrice said.

"Oh." She looked toward the window. The sun was already down, and she could hear a football skittering around the cobblestones of the courtyard below. "Enzo?"

"Mmhmm."

There were other voices, too. Male voices. Shouting something.

"*Mitto!*"

The skidding ball.

"*Mittere!*"

Another kick.

"*Misi.*"

"*Missus!*"

Fina frowned. "Is that...?"

"Gio invited Zeno over for Angela's dinner. I think he's going to the market with us later, too."

She sat up, totally forgetting that Beatrice's fangs had scared her. "Zeno's here? And they're—"

"Declining Latin verbs while they kick around a soccer ball? Yes. Yes, they are. My husband thinks Latin is God's language and everyone should know it."

Fina started laughing just as they started on *habeo.*

"My son, your husband, and Zeno are...They're being such...There is an English word, but I cannot remember."

"*Nerds,*" Beatrice said, joining in the laughter. "They are being really, really big nerds right now."

"Yes." She couldn't stop laughing. "Yes, that is the word."

Beatrice stood and walked to the window, where the kicking and shouting had ceased.

She waved at whoever she saw and said, "I think Zeno heard you laughing. He's got that hungry, dazed expression on his face."

And all of a sudden, she was thinking about fangs again. "Hungry?"

"Not the kind of hungry you're thinking."

She flushed and Beatrice laughed.

"Okay, *now* it's the kind of hungry you're thinking. Oh my, I bet he loves that blush you have."

"It's incredibly embarrassing. I've blushed since I was a girl. I hate it."

"You better get used to the fangs, Fina, because when this goes up—" she pointed the finger of her right hand straight "—these go down." The other hand came up, two fingers dropping like fangs.

"Oh." Well, that was more than she ever expected to know about vampire sex. "That's...interesting."

"Yes, it is." Beatrice grinned. "You and Zeno couldn't keep your eyes off each other last night. I noticed."

"Was I that obvious?" She paused, thought about what Beatrice had said. "It was more than just me?"

"Oh yeah. What kind of letters have you two been writing for the past couple years?" She waved out the window again, then pointed down and nodded. "Gio wants me to come down and meet them. I'll hold Zeno off from charging up the stairs until you're ready."

"Please do."

Why was she talking about this with her employer? But employers didn't break into your room and jump on your bed, excited about a discovery. They didn't call their husbands "nerds" while that husband was playing football with your son. They didn't tease you about a man—vampire—you were dangerously attracted to.

"Beatrice?"

She paused at the door. "Yeah?"

"Are we friends now?"

Beatrice smiled. "I'm trying to be. I don't do very well with the whole scary-vampire-lording-over-humans thing yet. Give me a few hundred years or so, and I'm sure I'll have it down."

Fina smiled. "I don't have many friends. I didn't want to assume."

"Assume away." She glanced down the hall. "But don't take long to get ready. Those boys are champing at the bit."

Fina didn't know exactly what that meant, but she quickly dressed and hurried downstairs.

And she did it wearing red lace under her clothes.

Well, Nonna, life certainly is interesting now.

Beatrice watched Zeno as Fina came down the stairs. The hungry look was back, but his cheeks had color, so she knew he'd fed recently. Smart of him. He must have sensed Fina was cautious about vampires, so he was being considerate and not taxing his self-control. Zeno was still talking with Enzo, debating soccer, which they both avidly followed. They shared a love for the same Italian club, and conversation seemed to swing between perfect excitement and utter despair. Often within the same sentence. When Fina came down, she joined them and the three talked like old friends while Beatrice watched from across the room.

Excellent. Things were progressing nicely.

Gio bent down and kissed her temple. "Happy, darling?"

"I'd be happier with presents." It was just so fun to annoy him about the present thing.

"You're hopeless."

"No, I'm present-less."

"You poor deprived girl."

"Have you ever thought about trying to steal Zeno away from the Vatican?"

He cocked his head at the change in subject. "Many times. He's a quiet sort, but I know for a fact he can take care of himself. Doesn't attract much attention, and he's a bulldog when it comes to research. He'd be an ideal employee. Previously, I'd not had anything to tempt him away from his comfortable cave in Rome, but now..."

She looked up at him innocently. "Look how helpful I'm being, meddling like this. You're so lucky to have me."

Giovanni smiled, his green eyes sparkling. "I know exactly how lucky I am. And I have to say, I approve. As long as Fina continues to like him, of course. I have no interest in replacing her, but I think she could use some help."

"He'd be perfect for it. And I'd breathe easier knowing that there was someone we trusted at the library. Someone stronger than a human."

"I've been thinking along the same lines." The humor fled Giovanni's face as he sat down next to her. "My reputation and Emil's protection have so far warned off anyone who might cause trouble, but as word of Andros's books spreads, I don't want to take chances. My sire's collection contains secrets I'm not even aware of. There could be others threatened by it. Even someone as well trained as Rudy would not be enough."

"So, Zeno or no Zeno, we need to find a vampire to live and work in Perugia."

"I think so."

She looked back at the pair, who were totally engaged.

"Well," she said, "hopefully this will end well for everyone."

"Let's get business out of the way, then go find some Christmas pipes for Enzo, eh?"

"Sounds good." She raised her voice a little. "Hey, let's go over what we found today, and then we'll eat."

All business, Zeno and Fina walked over to the dining room while Enzo drifted to the kitchen, uninterested in the "library stuff."

The excitement made Beatrice's blood run. She'd been on and off the phone all day with Dez in California and the priest whom Zeno had referred her to last night. What they'd put together brought Rafael's manuscript much closer than she ever would have expected.

"After we looked over the letters last night, I had my assistant in California look up some of the ship manifests and passenger lists we've collected from that period."

"Why did you collect those?" Fina asked. "Just curious."

"To examine what was being shipped in and out of California at the time. Most of our interest has actually been in the cargo, but I had Dez look for any passengers out of Monterey from 1803. We know that was the last letter that Rafael sent. Know that he told his friend he had a plan. So I started looking there."

"Meanwhile," Zeno said, "I asked a certain priest who specializes in genealogy to look into Father Pietro. There were only so many Franciscans named Pietro who came from prominent families in Rome during that time. And from his handwriting and vocabulary, he had more than a church education. Pietro came from wealth."

They all sat comfortably at the dining table, Giovanni and Beatrice on one side, Zeno and Fina on the other. Beatrice had to bite back a smile at how close the two were sitting to each other.

Zeno continued, "There was one Franciscan who stood out. The third son of a very prominent family, his brothers had taken over the estate, but he was educated for the church. Why he became a Franciscan, I do not know. But there were records of his family because they owned quite a lot of land and were minor nobility." Then he smiled. "And what we found is very interesting."

"A sister?" Fina asked. "Was there a sister?"

Zeno's eyes locked with hers. "How did you know?"

"I didn't. Just suspected. How else would Rafael have been so confident that Pietro could give

Antonia his message? She had to have been part of his family. A sister seemed the most likely."

"Very clever," Zeno said. "Yes, Pietro had a sister named Antonia. There was a mention of her marrying in 1805, but after that, we could find nothing. And nothing about the identity of who she married, either."

"So we don't know if they found their way back to each other?" Fina looked stricken.

"Not necessarily," Beatrice said. "Dez found him. There were numerous Rafaels who sailed from California in 1803 and 1804, but only one with a name that struck me. Rafael Szarka left the Presidio of Monterey in March of 1804. He sailed down to Mexico—well, Baja California—then back to Spain. After that, we have no idea."

"Szarka is not a Spanish name," Zeno said.

"No, it's Hungarian." Beatrice waved a hand. "Don't ask. I can't tell you. But this is our Rafael, I'm certain of it."

"So we know his name," Fina said. "And presumably, he went back to Spain. But we have no idea what happened after that."

Zeno squeezed her hand where it lay on the table. "We'll keep looking, *cara*. This much progress is already far more than I would expect to learn in such a short time."

Giovanni nodded. "Now, let's eat. Then we will go show Enzo the city at Christmastime." He put his arm around Beatrice. "I think we're all ready for a little fun."

Fina couldn't remember the last time she'd had so much fun. Giovanni and Beatrice dragged them all over Rome. They gaped at churches and piazzas decorated with thousands of lights. They visited the giant Christmas tree near the Colosseum. They wandered past the shops near the Spanish Steps and took in the toys and luxury fashions that decorated the store windows.

Spending time with Zeno was effortless. The more she knew him, the more she liked. Though she still hadn't caught a glimpse of the rumored fangs. He joked with Enzo, listening to everything the boy said, and appeared to truly enjoy their conversations, unlike some adults who only condescended to children. He took her arm with old-fashioned manners...but then, he *was* old-fashioned. He casually mentioned how Rome had changed over decades, but he still seemed to enjoy the modern lights and markets.

He was...perfect.

And he was a vampire. He would never die. Never grow older. She tried not to think too far ahead, but the simmering interest she'd nurtured for over years of correspondence had heated to a full, rolling boil. She wanted him. And she suspected he wanted her. But was it only a casual interest in a woman, or something more serious?

Fina didn't have casual affairs. In fact, Zeno spending time with Enzo broke one of her cardinal rules. The few men she'd dated over the years had never met her son. No relationship had become serious enough for that. But Enzo had already met the vampire, and she could see the hero worship starting to take hold. The boy had no paternal figures in his life—her own papa and brothers no longer acknowledged her—and she knew her son was hungry for male interaction, especially as he'd grown older. It was part of the reason he looked forward to Giovanni's visits.

"Fina." Zeno called her over to one stall as they strolled through the market of the Piazza Navona. "Look at these!"

He was laughing, holding up gaudy earrings with flashing Christmas lights on them, only to have them short out when he held them up to his ears. He grinned and pulled a few euro out of his pocket to give to the vendor.

"No," she protested. "Look. They're…" She started to laugh. "Well, they're awful, aren't they? And they don't even work, Zeno."

He leaned down and took her arm, whispering in her ear, "They probably did, *cara*. But vampires and electronics do not get along well, do they?"

"Oh?" Then she remembered. Beatrice had told her the current all immortals carried in their touch, called *amnis*, wreaked havoc on anything electronic. She wasn't sure why. She smiled up at Zeno. "And here I thought you were only a Luddite."

"Oh, I am. Computers are not my friend." He hadn't leaned away from her ear. "I prefer a hands-on approach when I want to research something."

Her heartbeat took off. He was so close. Just beside her neck, his breath tickling above her scarf. The perfect position to kiss her. Or bite her. She looked around for Enzo, but he was in a circle surrounding a couple of street musicians with Beatrice and Giovanni.

"*Cara mia...*," Zeno said gruffly. "Surely you know."

She could hardly breathe. "Yes."

"And would you?"

"It...depends."

He pulled a little away to look into her eyes, but his arm was still linked with her own. "On what does it depend?"

Were those fangs behind his lips? He was murmuring, but was it because he did not want her to see him?

"It's not that you're what you are, Zeno. Maybe a little, but it is more that..." She glanced over at Enzo again. "I do not bring people into my son's life who are casual. I rarely date and when I do—"

"Why would I be interested in *dating* you?"

Her heart plunged. Was that derision in his voice? How could she have been so wrong? Her face felt as if it was on fire.

"Dating," he continued, even as she looked for escape, "is a ridiculous modern concept. Why would I take you to the theater or the cinema once a week for months when I could work with you for one day and know you better? And I don't eat regular meals, not the kind you do. So dining is not an option. Dating is useless."

"But I—"

"We already suit each other, Fina. It was obvious before we even met."

Was she starting to see the side of him that was the "terror of the Vatican?" She could see his temper brewing.

"Zeno, I think we misunderstand each other."

"I am not interested in something casual. Do I look like a casual person?" His head swung around the marketplace. "I am older than everyone here, save Vecchio and that old vampire sitting by the fountain."

"There's a vampire by the fountain?" Her wide eyes looked over his shoulder.

"He's not dangerous—pay attention."

Her own temper piqued, she pulled her arm away and said, "I am not one of your assistants to order around, Zeno Ferrara. I may be a quiet person, but quiet does not equal meek."

"Are you afraid of me?" He stepped closer. "Is that what this is about?"

"No!"

"Then why do you step away from me?"

"I do not." Did she?

A pair of young men came up to them, clearly interested in the scene. She knew their type. Calling at the girls. Hungry to feed their ego with feminine embarrassment.

"Signorina, does he bother you?" one asked.

The other said, "Old brute, you should leave the lady alone." Then he laughed. "She is too pretty for you anyway. Signorina, run away with us! Leave the rude one. We know how to take care of a lady."

"Perhaps *both* of us can try," the other said, leering.

With a swiftness that was more than a little inhuman, Zeno turned to them. She could see the edge of his fangs when he gritted his teeth. He gripped both of them on the side of their necks and hissed, "Leave the piazza now, and do not ever speak to her again."

Without another word, both boys turned and left the square. They did not look at her. They did not turn back. There were no obnoxious comments thrown over their shoulders. It had all happened so quickly; no one in the crowd even turned to stare.

Speechless, she felt Zeno grab her hand. He pulled her to a secluded corner near the fountain, and she could see a cold-eyed man turn to watch them with narrowed eyes.

"Is that the vampire?" she whispered.

"Fina," he growled, raking his hand through his hair. "I am sorry. I have a possessive streak and—"

"Are we safe?"

"I would *never* hurt you."

"No, from that vampire over there."

He turned and hissed something in an unknown language. Slavic, perhaps? With a grim smile, the other immortal melted into the night.

"I'm sorry," he said again. "I promise—"

"Would you ever use your…whatever that was on me?" Her eyes felt huge, blinking as if to clear the frightening image from her mind. "Like you did on those boys?"

"Fina, no." He leaned his forehead against her temple and she felt it in her hand, like a trickling of warm water stealing up her arm. "Do you feel that, *cara?*" he whispered.

"Yes."

"That is *amnis.*"

"What you used on the boys."

"I can manipulate the human mind with it. I can move the earth with it. I feed it with mortal blood, and it keeps me alive, even after one hundred years on this earth."

She couldn't stop the shiver that overtook her. Zeno wrapped his arms around her shoulders and she felt it again, heating her skin. That warm trickle of energy spread over her limbs, as if an invisible blanket fell.

"I can use it to warm you. I can bring you extreme pleasure. But I will never use it to manipulate your will, Serafina. I promise you."

"How can I be certain?"

"Because I wish to use far more enjoyable methods of persuasion to convince you to accept me."

She looked up. "Accept you how?"

His dark brown eyes burned into hers. "As a lover. A friend. A part of your life. Your son's life."

"You do not wish to date me," she said breathlessly.

"We are beyond that. We know each other. Maybe not our bodies, because we have only just met. But my mind recognized yours. From the first letters. I have kept them all. Every one."

"I suspect you keep all your letters. Neatly filed. Organized by date and cross-referenced by mutual acquaintance."

A smile broke through his severe expression. "See? You do know me. But yours were the only ones I pulled out to read over and over. Trying to guess who you were from the angle of your signature. They stayed in my desk."

"I kept yours in my briefcase," she murmured.

"In the red-striped pocket?"

Her eyes went wide again. "How did you know?"

"Because I know you, too." He bent down, lips brushing over her forehead. "The girl with the fiery name and the careful signature. Cautious Fina."

Her heart was going to beat out of her chest.

"Loyal Fina," he whispered as his nose touched hers. "Beautiful Fina."

His lips pressed against her own and she leaned into him, opening her mouth as Zeno's hands came to cup the back of her head. Soft, searching kisses turned into deep tangles of tongue and lips and teeth. She felt them, growing long in his mouth, the fangs that had so frightened her.

She pressed closer, devouring him. Swallowing the groan that came from her throat. He tasted of heat and wine. The tip of her curious tongue reached up to caress the length of one fang and

Zeno growled into her mouth. His hands fisted in her hair.

"Stop," he said against her lips. "We must stop now or I will steal you away. Then Giovanni would burn me alive for kidnapping his best employee."

A strangled laugh from her mouth. "Oh yes. I'm sure."

"No, really. Burning is what he does to his enemies." His thumb brushed the edge of her mouth and when he pulled it away, she could see the smear of red. Had she cut her lip on his fangs? She hadn't felt a thing.

"The kissing." He closed full lips over the drop of her blood, then teased her with a glimpse of his tongue running over one fang. "Mmm. The kissing comes with practice."

"Oh." And there was her face. On fire again. Zeno smiled wickedly.

"You're beautiful, Fina. And your taste..." His eyes flicked over her body. "I can't wait for practice."

"Zeno—"

"When does Enzo go to sleep?"

"What? I...I don't—"

"I can be patient, but I don't want to be." He took a step back. "Do you need patience?"

Did she?

No.

She wanted him to heat her blood again. To make her feel alive in ways she hadn't since she'd become a mother. She wanted Zeno to see the red lace under her clothes. She wanted to know just what he meant by practice.

"He'll go to sleep as soon as we get home," she said. "It's very late."

"Good."

He grabbed her hand and pulled her back to the market stalls in the piazza, carols playing on pipes and flutes filling the air while they walked under twinkling gold lights. When they got back to Giovanni and Beatrice, she could see her son rubbing his eyes. Fina realized it was almost midnight.

"Time to go, I think," she said cheerfully. "Enzo, did you have fun?"

She saw her son eying Zeno's hand as he held hers. The vampire showed no sign of letting her go anytime soon. Nor did she want him to. Still, the public declaration made her a little nervous.

Enzo looked from his mother's flushed face to Zeno, then back again. He smiled. "Yes. Very fun. But Gio was right. Some of those pipers were just terrible."

CHAPTER FOUR

Zeno sat back, leaning against the stone walls that lined the courtyard, closing his eyes as he listened to the comforting sounds of a family retiring for the night. He heard Angela's quiet snores in the downstairs bedroom. The guard's unobtrusive footsteps. Enzo's sleepy murmurs from the second story. Beatrice whispering something just past Zeno's hearing as she and Fina talked in the hall.

Giovanni came to stand beside him, holding out a glass of red wine. "You still don't take spirits, am I correct?"

He shook his head. "Too strong. Wine is all I can handle."

Zeno was still young for an immortal, with the keen senses that had not been dulled by centuries. While older vampires like Giovanni could enjoy the brandy or whisky he'd consumed as a human, his taste was still too sensitive. The heavy red wine, with its hints of earth and smoke and mushroom, was as complex as he could handle.

"Mmm," he said after the first sip. "My thanks. This is excellent."

"Do you need to speak to me?"

He curled one corner of his mouth up in a rueful smile. "Do I?"

Giovanni sat on the bench across from him. "She is under my aegis, Ferrara."

"Ah, I forget how old-fashioned you are."

"Not old-fashioned. Cautious."

Zeno shrugged. "You know I am a bastard. I have no sire and no political allegiance."

"You live in Rome, but work within the Church. I will admit that Emil Conti may not have required a formal pledge from you—"

"He has not."

"But that does not mean he has overlooked you. You could be an asset to him. He's aware of it."

"Conti's not a bad sort." He took another sip of wine. "But I have no interest in politics and power plays. I never have."

Giovanni finally smiled. "Why do you think I like you so much?"

"I desire her, Giovanni." All amusement fled his expression. "More than desire."

"If she is willing, I have no objection to a liaison, of course. If your interest lies further—"

"I think it does."

Giovanni raised a skeptical eyebrow. "Think?"

"It does, dammit." He frowned and raked a hand through his hair. He really did need that haircut.

"Zeno—"

"I lost my temper in the market like a newly turned child," he said. "I thought of her when I had only her letters to hold. And now that I have met her in the flesh…"

"She's a lovely woman."

A bitter laugh escaped him. "For the first time in one hundred twenty years, there is something I want to possess. And I haven't even slept with the woman yet. You know how this instinct will be once I have her."

Giovanni opened his mouth, then closed it. He thought for a moment before he spoke. "I do not know her well. I suspect you know more of her, though you've only just met in person. But I will say this: She is human. Do not waste time. The years stretch out before us, centuries with which to pace ourselves. She does not have that. She's young. But every second is precious."

"Do you object to our relationship?"

"Not at all."

"Thank you."

"I'm not her father, only her employer. And her necessary protector in our world." Giovanni smiled slowly. "Unless she has another, of course. You know the offer still stands."

"I cannot abandon my work."

"So don't." He sipped his whisky. "Take your precious letters with you. Or borrow them in batches to work on in Perugia. I'm sure you can persuade or bully Arturo into it. God knows you've scared away all the suitable assistants in Rome. There is more than enough room for both of you to work in the library there. She's alone, Zeno. Think about it. I need to hire someone to watch over her and the library. Wouldn't you like it to be you and not someone else?"

He paused, knowing that to take Giovanni's offer would change the balance of his eternity.

"I'll think about it."

He saw a light go on in Fina's bedroom on the third floor.

Giovanni stood and said, "Don't waste a minute."

Zeno set the unfinished glass of wine on the stone bench and walked into the house, up the three flights of stairs that led to her room, quietly conscious of the sleeping humans around him. They would not hear him. And he heard no sign of Giovanni and Beatrice. They had fled the property, affording Zeno and Fina privacy.

He tapped softly on the door, and she opened it. Her cheeks were delightfully flushed with the redness that so often marked them. She probably hated it, but it delighted him. Her lips looked like she'd been worrying them between her teeth.

"Invite me in," he whispered, tamping down his hunger.

She frowned. "Do I need to do that?"

"Yes." The innocent question made him grin. "But not for any supernatural reasons."

"Oh." She opened the door wider. "Please. Come in, Zeno."

He walked through the door and quickly turned, setting the lock for privacy. He held his finger to his lips as he walked toward her.

"Quiet," he whispered. Finally reaching her, he leaned down and brushed a kiss across her lips. "We must be quiet."

She clutched at the lapels of his coat, but he tugged it off. Then his shirt. He toed off his shoes. And while he did that, she started to undo the buttons on her blouse. He put a hand up to stop her.

"Why?" she said.

"I like to unwrap my own presents."

She smiled and let him slip the buttons loose to reveal dark red lace that barely covered her. It was the color of wine. Of blood. He grew even harder than he'd been, and his fangs fell in his mouth.

"Fina," he groaned as his mouth tasted the lace.

"Red for luck," she said.

"My luck or yours?"

"Both, I think."

He fought his instincts to take, take, *take* as he slipped the lace aside to taste her skin. Though he knew how to make his bite pleasurable, he did not want to try it their first time together. It might be too shocking, and he had plans to ensnare his little human quite thoroughly into his world.

"*Cara mia,*" he whispered, pushing her back toward the bed. "We must be quiet, but I do not want to be."

"This time," she said, quieting him with her lips. *This time.*

He smiled into her kiss, the possessive instincts assuaged. There would be a next time. And a next.

In fact, Fina might not know it, but Zeno decided in that moment he had no intention of letting her go.

She laid herself before him, baring her body in the moonlight, and Zeno realized it was entirely different kind of possession when the object of your desire offered herself. He had given up every worldly object in order that those *things* might not own him. But he surrendered himself to her arms, happy to claim Fina as his own.

"Mine," he whispered as he kissed down her body. The words didn't feel grasping or controlling. They were sweet on his tongue.

Because, in fact, she was the one who possessed.

He tasted her skin. The sweet arousal between her thighs. Fina's fingers clenched in his hair as she gasped with pleasure, and he decided perhaps he didn't need a haircut after all, because the quick pleasure-pain made him focus.

Focus.

She was soft. Mortal. He had to be careful. He heard her heart pounding. Could feel the rush of her blood.

When he finally entered her, he could not hide the fangs that grew long in his mouth, even when he tried. He turned his head to the side but felt her hand pressing his cheek, forcing his gaze back to her. Forcing his lips to meet hers in a searing kiss.

"Fina."

"I do not fear you, Zeno."

He thrust harder, for every part of her accepted him in that moment. Fina stroked his fangs, cutting her tongue on the edge of them. Zeno took it. He only had so much control, after all. He sucked her tongue in his mouth, tasting the sweet tang of her blood. Like a drop of the finest wine, it slid down his throat.

Seconds later, she came again. A few moments after that, Zeno followed her.

And it was a lovely fall.

Giovanni held Beatrice's hand as they walked through the gate and into the courtyard. It was only a few hours before dawn, and they'd spent most of the night running around Rome, racing each other from one Christmas tree to the next and playing tag in the Piazza San Pietro like giddy children. More than one of Rome's numerous immortals saw them. None commented on their mad behavior.

Sometimes it was good to be a terribly feared monster.

Beatrice tilted her head and bit back a smile. "Wow. That's energy, Zeno."

"They're still…?" He tried not to laugh. "Indeed they are."

"I think it's been a long time for both of them."

He gave her his most pitiful expression. "For me as well, Tesoro."

She calculated in her head. "Really? Ten hours?"

"Practically an eternity."

"That's what you get for not giving me presents in a timely fashion, you insatiable man."

He reached down and palmed his wife's firm backside, caressing one of his favorite personal landmarks. "I am insatiable. Are you complaining?"

"No," she said, tugging him into the house and running to their room.

He tackled her just inside the door. Then, ignoring the faint cries of their guests' pleasure, he set about sating the hunger their playful romp through the city had aroused. After, when she lay boneless against his chest, he let his eyes close, content to slip into day rest as he felt the tiny pulls of the sun.

"Gio?"

"Hmm?"

"You never answered me the other day."

He frowned and opened his eyes. "About what?"

"What would you have done if I hadn't wanted to become immortal?"

The dark swept down. "Why do you ask this? It is a pointless question."

"I want to know."

He rolled away. "Beatrice—"

"Would you have left me when I got too old?"

He spun around, eyes wide. "What? No. Why would you even ask me that?"

She shrugged. "I just...I was thinking about Zeno and Fina. And Natalie, too."

"I believe Natalie will turn when their children are old enough. Why are you asking me this?"

"Why won't you answer?"

Because the black memories fell over him. And they were heavy. So heavy.

"What do you want to hear?" he asked in a rough voice. "You want to hear that I would have watched you grow old? Raging silently at the loss of the one woman I have ever loved? That I would have counted the minutes and seconds of your life? Agonized over every stupid human way you could be killed?"

"Gio—"

"Do you want to know how I thought about it? Before you had decided on a life with me? When you were still mortal and *so* vulnerable? That often the darkness grew so black that I almost begged Tenzin to turn you *without your consent* because your fury would have been nothing to your death?"

"I'm sorry," she said, crawling to him and throwing her arms around his neck. "You're right. It was a stupid question. I'm sorry, Gio. I'm sorry."

She kept apologizing, but he stopped listening. He only wanted to hold her. Wanted to feel the strength of her arms. The touch of her *amnis* as her energy twined around his. He let his head fall on her shoulder.

She would be more powerful than him one day. The richness of her blood was evident, even in her youth. The thought did not threaten him. It reassured him.

"I would have loved you every minute I was allowed," he whispered. "And I hope you would have never known how much it hurt to lose you. I would have wanted only joy. Only peace. And when you were gone, I would have let myself burn. Because I have lived a long time, and the centuries were too weary without you."

Her arms tightened around his neck.

"Don't die, Gio. Don't ever leave me alone."

"Never." He pulled her head back to kiss her. "We are eternal."

Zeno needed to seek shelter, but he did not want to leave Fina. She lay in his arms, naked and languid with pleasure. He'd exhausted her and he did not feel the least bit sorry. He only wished they'd been in a more private location, because he wanted her sweet cries to fill the room. He wondered if the lightproof quarters in Perugia were soundproofed, as well.

A valid question before accepting a job offer.

"Zeno." She stretched out her legs, her toes tickling his legs. "Do you need to leave?"

He glanced at the clock. "I have time. Do you want me to go so you can sleep?"

She shook her head. "Tell me about your life."

"I know about my life, I'd rather hear about yours."

"You have more stories."

He chuckled. "I cannot argue with that. I was born in Naples."

"What year?"

"1893."

"Old man."

"But rather young for a vampire. My family was very common. Fishermen. And I wanted nothing to do with it. I had very grand aspirations, and a very good education, actually. But I went to war."

"World War One?"

"Yes, I ran off to join as soon as I could. Stupid child. But I found that I was a rather good soldier." He smiled. "When the war was over, I also found the card skills I'd learned while I waited around for battle came in handy."

She lifted her head. "You were a gambler?"

"Yes, a good one." He shook his head. "I made a lot of money. But after a time, the games, taking the money from boys and men who couldn't afford it, began to wear on me. It wasn't challenging. I turned my mind to business. Or what I called business. I loaned money to disreputable people, which was profitable, but violent. I had money. Women. Automobiles and houses. But I could not go home. I would have shamed my mother."

"So you joined the church?"

"I hated it all. By the time I was thirty-five, I hated myself. I was cynical and angry. So I thought…" He shrugged. "I will give this all away. Give it to God. All of it. Even myself. Perhaps He could do something with this wreck of a man and his gains from so much suffering. It was impetuous, but I followed through with it. During the second war, it was a good place to be, even though Rome did not do enough." He clenched his teeth.

"Not nearly enough. But still, I was able to move people who needed to be moved. Hide those who needed hiding."

"You were part of the resistance."

"The collar protected me. And the sisters." He grinned. "Never underestimate the fierce compassion of our Catholic sisters. There were many hidden in the convent who had never read a prayer book in their life. But they hid them. Many of them. And then...I became a vampire, but that is a story for another time. It was not as pleasant as joining the church."

She was looking at him with an awed expression. "You are a brave man, Zeno Ferrara."

"I don't know that I'm all that brave."

"Those who are not afraid of change are brave. And you have not only survived change, you have searched for it when life was not what you wanted. That is brave."

"Are you brave?"

She wrinkled her brow. "I don't know. I try to be."

"Cautious Fina."

"Caution is wisdom, isn't it? Life is unexpected. You have to be prepared for anything. I didn't expect to fall in love with my pig of a professor and become pregnant with Enzo, but I did. I was *not* cautious. And so I learned to be. And having my son was the best thing in my life. So unexpected!" A sweet smile crossed her lips. "I did not imagine my family would cut me off as they did, but I learned from it.

And now I am independent, not leaning on them for my security. And I'm happier for it. Yes, caution is wisdom."

"Not fear?"

She shook her head and her quiet strength humbled him. "I don't think so, no."

"I think you are brave."

"I think you are very flattering."

"Am I allowed?"

"Yes, you are allowed." She rolled over and put her head on his chest. "Your heart beats."

"Sometimes, yes. Not always."

"And you did not bite me when we made love."

"Not this time, no."

"Where do you get your blood?"

"I drink mostly donated blood, but get it as fresh as I can. It loses potency for us the longer it is dead."

"Hmm." She frowned. "Did you not want to drink from me?"

He stroked over her head and down to her neck. "Oh yes. I want that very much."

"But you did not."

"I didn't want to scare you."

"Does it hurt?" she asked.

"Not unless I want it to. If I bit you, you would feel extreme pleasure."

She pursed her lips. "I think I have much to learn about vampires." Then she whispered, "Hands-on research might be necessary."

Zeno laughed as he twined a lock of her brown hair around his finger. "Do you know I could fall in love with you, Serafina Rossi?"

"That seems fair, since I feel the same way," she said, her eyes warming him even more than her body. "Life is quite unexpected, isn't it?"

CHAPTER FIVE

Fina sat next to Zeno with Enzo on her other side. They had decided to attend the Pope's midnight mass—which was actually a ten-o'clock mass—on Christmas Eve. The tourists had poured into Rome, seemingly all at once. Flooding the markets and filling the streets, they spoke in every language imaginable, the lure of the Eternal City tempting people from all around the world.

But within the basilica, Fina felt peace spill over her. It was crowded, but Zeno had been able to acquire three tickets to sit inside the church. Ancient songs filled the air, along with the smell of incense. Latin chants rang over myriad whispers in every language. She was reminded of her childhood, of Nonna's lace-covered head and scratchy Christmas dresses. The electric lights of Rome were beautiful, but it was the dripping candles near the altar that spoke Christmas to her.

She felt Zeno tense beside her.

"What is it?"

He leaned down to her ear. "There are many vampires here."

"Should we be concerned? I thought there were always many immortals in Rome."

"There are." He glanced over Fina's head to check Enzo, whose eyes were barely open.

"So why—"

"I did not have a woman and child before. I did not notice them as much."

She slipped her hand into his, and he gripped it. "You're going to be insufferably possessive for a while, aren't you?"

He grunted. "Possibly forever." Zeno's eyes narrowed on someone or something on the other side of the church. After several minutes, she felt him relax again. "Damn Catholic vampires," he muttered.

"Aren't you a Catholic vampire?"

"I'm young. Nostalgia is to be expected. The old ones cause me more concern."

"Shhh," she said, leaning into his side. "Listen."

The Pope had started his address, his solemn voice filling the marble and gold-clad church. For hours, the crowd sat in silence, kneeling in prayer or listening to the beautiful songs that filled the air. Occasionally intoning when the liturgy called for their response.

She clutched Zeno's hand, thinking about how much had changed over the years of his long life. And what had stayed the same. It made sense to her, despite his earlier complaint, that so many immortals clung to the traditions of the church. Whether they were devout or not, those traditions would be familiar.

The mass passed without vampire disruption, despite Zeno's worries. It was only the three of them, as Giovanni and Beatrice had decided to celebrate at the Pantheon, which was near the house and did not attract as many tourists. As they filed out of the church, she felt Zeno's callused hand grip her own. Saw his arm drape over Enzo's shoulders as he guided them through the crowd. The mood was festive, but people were tired, ready to head to quiet homes and beds, and they found their way back to their neighborhood quite easily.

The previous days had been filled with sightseeing and shopping. Enzo, Angela, Rudy, and Fina had toured the city during the day and prepared the house for Christmas, always taking long afternoon naps so they could enjoy the night with their vampire hosts. Both nights, Zeno had joined them, earning some playful ribbing from Giovanni for his sudden disinterest in work.

But he *had* been working. She knew when Zeno left her, deep in the night after hours of talking and loving, he returned to his cavernous workroom in the Vatican, searching for clues to the mystery of the disappearing Franciscan and his Antonia. Many of their whispered conversations were not the teasing exchanges of lovers, but the polite—and sometimes contentious—debate of colleagues. And though she hadn't returned to the Vatican Library, Fina still felt a part of the research.

She loved it.

Zeno still had not bitten her, and Fina wondered whether it was her own hesitance that stopped
him, or if it was Zeno's struggle with his possessive
nature that made him pause. He was, as Giovanni
had teased her, a man of great passion. And energy.
She'd never felt the complete focus of a lover as
she did with Zeno. But still, she wondered what
would happen when she returned to Perugia and he
remained in Rome.

"What are you stewing about, *cara?*"

"Hmm?" She looked up to see him watching her
face with a frown. "I'm just tired. Don't glare."

"I'm not glaring."

Fina broke into a laugh. "You are a cranky old
man, Zeno Ferrara."

"I am a dangerous creature, Signorina. You
would do well to remember." Despite the harsh
words, his eyes laughed at her.

"How could I forget?" She shivered, and Zeno
pulled her closer.

He *was* dangerous. She could see it lurking in
the edges of his eyes at times, especially when they
walked around the city. Could see it in the sweep of
his eyes or the occasional way her hair stood on end
when he was near. Sometimes, she knew he sensed
threats around them, but he was careful to shield
her, even from the awareness of it.

Fina, knowing her own inexperience in the
immortal world, did not press the issue. While she
had no desire to live in ignorance, she also suspected that being with Zeno put her in the path of

those who could harm her and her son without a second thought. She had no foolish desire to fight Zeno's protective instincts if he was keeping Enzo from harm.

"What are you doing after you leave us?"

He lifted the corner of his mouth. "Who said I am leaving?"

"Weren't you going back to—"

"It's Christmas, Fina." He grinned. "Even my library is closed."

"Oh."

"Giovanni and Beatrice offered one of the lightproof rooms in their home," he said. "For the holiday."

She smiled as Enzo asked, "We'll see you on Christmas then, Zeno?"

"Yes. More Latin lessons tomorrow night," Zeno joked. "No doubt Gio thinks I could use a review."

Beatrice tried not to let her Cheshire grin show too much during Christmas dinner. After all, she was sure that, at some point, Zeno and Fina would have met without her machinations. Probably. It wouldn't have been as perfect as this, though.

Fina and Enzo, charming single mother and son. Alone for so many years. Happy, but incomplete. Zeno, a cranky loner who thought no one would understand him or welcome him. Two lonely people with uncommon interests, finding each other during a magical Christmas in Rome.

Oh yeah. She was good.

"You're looking very smug, Tesoro." Gio lowered himself into the leather chair next to her.

"That's because I am. Very smug."

"I will admit, they are well suited."

Beatrice snorted. "Please. They're perfect for each other. Has he given you an answer about Perugia yet?"

"Not yet. I wonder if he's asked Fina for her opinion. It would be a big change. And it seems fast."

"Fast? Kind of yes. But they've been writing to each other for two years. So it doesn't seem that fast to me."

He shrugged. "I suppose you're correct."

Beatrice shook her head. "It's still so hard for you to admit that, isn't it?"

"Torturous." He leaned toward her. "Though… will you admit that I was correct to send Brother Pietro's letters to Perugia?"

Her mouth dropped open. "No! They belong—"

"Because if I had not…" His lips trailed up to her ear. "…who would have orchestrated such a perfect match, my love?"

"You're kind of evil."

"Admit you're glad I did it."

She mashed her lips together, only to hear him laugh.

"Fine," she finally said. "Fine. Though you were completely *wrong* to misfile my letters, the situation was salvaged by my stellar matchmaking skills."

"That's as much of a concession as I'm going to get, isn't it?"

"Yep."

"Fine. I suppose you're tired of arguing about the letters, aren't you?"

"It's Christmas." She leaned over and pressed a kiss to his cheek. "Even though it doesn't feel like it without presents. Let's not work."

"Presents come on Epiphany. I've told you."

"Whatever." She was still prepared to sulk. A little.

"So if we're not working," he started, "should I wait to tell you I've found Rafael and Antonia?"

"*What?*"

Fina tried to maintain her professional persona as they drove out of the city, staring out the windows of the hired car as city lights gave way to scattered houses. But she was excited. Never before had she participated in a search like this. Most of her career was spent in quiet offices and workrooms, or searching online or through catalogues.

But this! She felt as if she were in a mystery novel.

"Excited?" Zeno asked, sitting next to her and watching her with the hint of a smile.

"Yes." She was buzzing.

He chuckled and pulled her hand into his lap.

The winery a small family operation, was situated about one hundred kilometers from Rome in the hills outside of Priverno. It was a small estate, but an old one. The same family had owned it and farmed it for over two hundred years.

And Giovanni was positive it had been founded by the former Franciscan calling himself Rafael Szarka.

They pulled through the gates just after eight o'clock, the lights of the small tavern lit at the front of the house. The winery was on the same property as the house, with bare vines crawling up the hills dotted with oaks and olive trees. The tavern served the estate's wine, along with a small selection of dishes for those requiring a meal. Giovanni had called the night before and the owner of the winery had been delighted to entertain a party from Rome, even at such a late hour.

As Fina stepped out of the car, she could see the signs of a building in decay. Though the vines they'd passed had been expertly tended and the rows spotless, she could see the creeping evidence of poverty. A broken border in the small garden. The sign hanging on a clumsily mended chain.

Villa Antonia.

"Signore Rosati, I must guess." Giovanni greeted the man who stepped out of the house.

"Yes, yes! Welcome. My wife has a dinner prepared for you with all the wine you would like. Come." The barrel-chested man held a hand toward the door of the stone-walled tavern. "We don't often get parties from Rome this time of year."

"Thank you for accommodating us," Fina said. "Everything smells delicious."

It did. And the table before them was loaded with traditional country fare. Cured meats and cheeses.

Crusty breads and dried fruit. A stew of some kind sat in the center of the table, steam trickling from the sides of the heavy lid.

She gaped. Since she was the only one with a normal appetite, Fina wondered just how much she was going to have to eat in order not to offend their hosts.

"I hope you're hungry," Zeno said quietly.

"We should have brought Enzo."

"You're right. That boy would be able to swallow half the table in one sitting."

He pulled out a chair for her and the four of them sat down.

"Signore Rosati," Beatrice asked in softly accented Italian. "We were hoping you and your wife would join us for dinner."

The man pouring wine at the counter looked confused. "But—"

"We have a confession," Giovanni added with a charming smile. "We are not only tourists, but historical researchers. Signore Ferrara, my friend, works for the Vatican Library, in fact."

"Researchers?" Signora Rosati had joined her husband. "What are you researching?"

Fina said, "We'd like to know more about the history of the estate. We understand it has been in the same family for many years."

"Two hundred," Signore Rosati boomed. "My wife's family is very well-known for their vines. I was only lucky enough to marry her." He winked at Fina as he poured her glass.

Fina felt Zeno tense and put a hand on his knee. "Really?" she whispered.

"I'll get it under control."

She let him scoot closer and wondered if the possessiveness would eventually get annoying. For now, it was amusing, and she hoped he'd be able to temper his instincts with time. She'd be more concerned if she didn't sense his own frustration.

"You are lucky my sister is visiting for the holidays," Signora Rosati said. "If you want to know about history, she is the one to ask. She keeps all the family papers and things like that."

Fina perked up. "She is visiting? Would she join us for dinner then? There is plenty to eat."

"And the wine will be far more enjoyable," Zeno said, "if we know more about it, Signore."

More confused smiles and quick conversations followed, but soon the two Rosatis and their sister, an older woman who introduced herself as Luisa, had joined them. Friendly conversation followed as food was served and wine flowed. Luckily, a very friendly spaniel had crawled under the table and the three vampires with small appetites were able to smuggle her some of their food.

Fina wondered how the three other people didn't notice that the vampires sat among them, chatting like common tourists. Their faces were fair, but the low tavern light hid Giovanni's pallor. Zeno, she presumed, had been more olive skinned in life, which was his advantage as an immortal. Their movements were just a bit too quick to her eyes. Their teeth gleamed, and their eyes were too keen.

But then, she had ignored the prickling feeling that Lorenzo had induced. Ignored her instincts because no common explanation could be had. Humans simply did not look beyond the obvious, unless they were forced to.

"So, Giovanni, Beatrice," Luisa asked, "what is it you are researching? The estate has many stories."

"We're curious about the founder," Beatrice said. "Who was he?"

Luisa grinned. "And you pick the most scandalous story! In truth, we did not know for many years what the truth was. There were rumors, of course. Because when our ancestor arrived in the region, he had no tie to it. No family or friends. He appeared with a pretty young wife and chest full of gold."

Zeno leaned an elbow on the table and sipped his wine. "Really? A chest full of gold?"

Luisa nodded. "That is the story. He bought the property and settled here. He'd brought some of his vines with him. Foreign vines, which was also scandalous to the locals, and he tended them himself. He had servants, but he worked with them. Not like a lord or a wealthy man at all. Rafael Szarka was a most unusual man for his time."

Fina said, "Szarka is not an Italian name."

"It's not." Luisa leaned forward, the delight evident on her face. "It is Hungarian. It was assumed by most of the town that he was *ungherese*, a Hungarian who had fled his homeland for some reason. But his wife, Antonia, was Italian. Though nobody knew from where."

"They married," Fina said. "They had a family."

Luisa cocked her head. "Oh yes. They had three children. Fifteen grandchildren. And after that, the family spread. But always, some stayed with the estate, taking care of the vines. Making the wine."

"It's a lovely story," Giovanni said. "But why did you call it a scandal?"

"Well, within the family, there has always been some question of how Rafael ended up with that chest of gold. And where on earth he came from. Was he a noble bastard? A thief? Someone who had to flee in disgrace of a scandal? It has been the cause of many family stories, as you can imagine."

Signore Rosati said, "My vote was always that he was a pirate."

"And how would a pirate know how to make wine?" his wife asked with a laugh before she turned back to the table. "The mystery was solved only a few years ago. One of the old stone barns on the estate was falling down. It had been falling down for many years and only the children went to play on the rocks. But it was getting dangerous for some of the little ones. So some of my cousins and my husband went out and pulled it down. And when they were clearing away the rocks for a new wall, they found a chest of old papers and a few pieces of clothes. Very, very old."

"A sea chest!" Signore Rosati said. "I was so hopeful. But sadly…not a pirate."

"There was a journal, though. In very good condition," Luisa said. "I was amazed. I was more amazed that it was written in Spanish and not Hungarian!"

Beatrice was practically jumping over the table. "Where is the journal now? What did you do with it?"

"I could not read it at all. It was in Spanish. *Old* Spanish. I took it to a history professor in Naples, where I work. He was fascinated, of course. He asked to photograph it for his records and said he would offer a translation if he could publish an article about the manuscript. I said yes, of course. He begged me to let him put it in the university library, but…"

Signora Rosati smiled. "It is our family history. It didn't seem right to give it away."

"The professor told me how to store it. Keep it well preserved. I have it in my home library," Luisa said.

Zeno asked, "And the translation?"

"The *scandalous* part. It turns out that Rafael Szarka was not a pirate, but a *priest*. He'd run away from the church when he fell in love with Antonia. She was from a very prominent family, but gave everything up to marry him."

"All the girls in the family loved that part," Signora Rosati said. "So romantic! He had traveled all the way from New Spain. From the missions in California. They came here under the name Szarka and stayed. In those days, of course, it would have been easy to change your name. They simply married and Antonia took his. There's no mention of her family ever bothering them."

Luisa said, "Much of the journal was about his life in California. Lots of technical information about wine cultivation."

"Quite interesting," Signore Rosati said. "We still use many of the pruning methods here in the vineyard that he did two hundred years ago. There are maps and diagrams of which vines grow best in different kinds of soil. Many things about grape cultivation that would have been very advanced for his time. It almost reads like a textbook."

"But with quite explicit notes in the margins," Luisa said with a grin. "There are other drawings other than vine diagrams. Rafael was quite an accomplished artist, as well as a farmer. I have to assume he and Antonia knew each other rather *well* before he went to California. Or he had a very good imagination."

Beatrice said, "I somehow think he left those parts out of the copies he sent around to the Franciscans."

"Most likely," Giovanni said with a smile. "Poor Father Ignacio."

Luisa's ears perked up. "There are other copies?"

"We think so," Beatrice said. "We're not sure. We have a series of letters written between Rafael and Antonia's brother, who was also a priest. That is how we tracked down his name."

"Oh, I would love to see them."

Fina said, "I'll make sure to send you copies. The letters are in Rome right now."

"And you managed to find our ancestor from only some letters?" Signora Rosati asked. "That is amazing."

"We had a lot of help," Beatrice told her. "Signore Ferrara is a letter expert."

"I am," Zeno said with a decisive nod.

Fina bit back a smile. So modest, her vampire.

"Well…thank you so much!" Luisa said. "Thank you for finding us. We all think it's such a beautiful story. Are you going to write some kind of book or paper about them?"

"Actually…" Giovanni leaned his forearms on the table. "We have ulterior motives for searching you out."

Luisa said, "You want to examine Rafael's journal?"

"Of course," her sister said. "Perhaps take pictures for your research. I'm sure that will be fine."

"More than that," Giovanni said. "We have been authorized to make you an offer for the purchase of the journal. We are not only researchers, but we work as agents for very discreet collectors around the world. Collectors who, I assure you, make the preservation of manuscripts such as Rafael's one of their highest priorities."

Beatrice said, "Our client is a private individual with an interest in history relating to wine. He had heard of your ancestor's journal only through rumors. We were hired to find it and buy it for him. I can assure you, it is for his own collection. And he will have no objection to the professor or your family keeping copies of the work. But he wants the original journal for his collection."

"Why?" Signore Rosati said. "It's unusual and interesting, but why would he want to buy it?"

"It is not my job to ask," Beatrice said, spreading her hands across the table. "I am only hired to find the books and broker the sale."

"But…" Luisa looked stricken. "We cannot sell it. It is our family history. We must—"

"How much?" Signora Rosati asked quietly.

Fina looked around the room again. It was a beautiful old room. A beautiful old house, built from the hill stones and weathered by time. But she could also see the signs of deterioration. This family could use the money.

Giovanni said, "Subject to our examination of the manuscript and its authentication, our client is prepared to offer you three million euros."

Jaws dropped around the table and an audible gasp was heard. Fina was flabbergasted. Early nineteenth-century journals, even rare ones, would be auctioned off for a fraction of that sum. Who on earth was their client? And why was he willing to pay so much?

Signora Rosati gripped her sister's hand, and Luisa nodded.

"Sold."

EPILOGUE

Los Angeles, California
One month later

The Hungarian sat down in Beatrice's private study, holding the precious journal with silk-gloved hands. He was a thin vampire with ascetic features and cold eyes. Beatrice had no idea how old he was, but his skin was extraordinarily pale, especially against his black hair and eyes. He paged through the journal as a man reads a book, a thin smile touching his lips occasionally as he traced the line of a drawing on the vellum.

The journal was remarkably intact, no doubt preserved by the sea chest it had been stowed in, which Beatrice had also been able to examine. The book was also very finely made, the vellum pages bound carefully and protected by a calf-skin cover. The ink was faded, but the illustrations Rafael had wrought between the notes on grape cultivation were clear.

The Franciscan had been a gifted artist. Portraits of Antonia, drawn from memory, filled almost half the book. Often her curling hair entwined with tendrils of the vines he'd drawn on the page. There were also numerous landscapes and scenes of mission life, but the most detailed drawings were of his lover.

"We were fortunate that it was in such excellent condition," she said.

"It is as if I can see him writing the words on the pages even now," her client said softly. "Drawing her. How very strange."

"Were you his benefactor?"

He angled his head slightly and she could see the lift of his brow. The Hungarian thought her impertinent. Oh well. Lots of older vampires did. Luckily, Beatrice's pedigree and connections—as well as her own reputation—protected her from most offense.

"His benefactor?" He looked back at the journal. "Of a sort."

"He returned to Europe a very wealthy man."

"Wealth is relative, of course. You say he married the woman."

"He did. They had three children and fifteen grandchildren. A very large extended family now. They still live on the estate and are far more comfortable after the sale of the journal."

The Hungarian closed the journal. "He would be pleased. Thank you, Ms. De Novo. Your work on this was excellent and your fee will be transferred to your account within the hour."

"Of course." She rose and saw him to the entryway, the manuscript stored in the box she'd brought from Rome and carried by the human who had waited in the hall.

"Please give my regards to your mate." The client bowed with the old world formality so many vampires preserved. "Perhaps the next time I am in America, we may meet."

"Of course. May I ask a question?"

"You may ask." He straightened the collar of his coat after Caspar helped him with it. Unspoken was the other half of the answer.

You can ask, but I probably won't answer.

"Why?"

"Why did I want it?" He examined her with those painfully cold eyes. There was a flicker for only a second, then they were flat and emotionless again. "Sometimes, Ms. De Novo, a person can save a life without even realizing it."

"Did Rafael save yours?"

He paused, and the thin smile touched his lips for another second. Then he angled his head down in another slight bow.

"Good night, Ms. De Novo. I'll send word if I have need of your services again."

Rome, Italy
The following Christmas

The shouts of Latin verbs and the skidding ball mingled with laughter from the courtyard as Ben and Enzo tried to keep the ball away from Zeno, who had promised to remain at human speed for the duration of the game. Christmas in Rome that year wasn't nearly as low-key as it had been the last.

"I haven't had time to talk with you much," Beatrice said, sitting at the kitchen table next to Fina, who was cutting vegetables for dinner as Angela fussed over the stove.

"You haven't," the once-reserved librarian said with a smile. "What interesting book mysteries have you and Gio solved lately?"

"Nothing quite so fun as Rafael's journal."

"That *was* fun. I often wonder where it is now. Why your client wanted it so much. I've enjoyed examining the digital copy."

"Don't let Zeno hear that," Beatrice teased. "A *digital* copy? The horror."

She laughed. There was a flush in Fina's cheeks. A quiet contentment that had added depth to her features.

"And how are things in Perugia?" Beatrice asked. "We're looking forward to our visit after New Year's."

"Things are going splendidly, though Zeno tried to appropriate an entire bookcase in the Greek section to keep magnifying glasses and dusting powders." She shook her head. "Incorrigible man."

Beatrice could easily imagine Zeno's temper butting up against the quiet determination of his partner. Fina would likely win every time, simply because Zeno didn't seem to be able to refuse her anything. They hadn't married or taken any traditional vows, but as far as she knew, the vampire and his human partner hadn't been separated for a single night since they officially met.

Zeno had moved to Perugia and taken residence in one of the lower rooms of the villa while Fina and Enzo remained in the house on the property. He'd bullied the administrators of the Vatican library into letting him take many of his letters with him, arguing that no one else was really interested in his research and he'd bring them back eventually.

Beatrice was guessing they agreed just to get rid of him.

He had also taken on some of the responsibilities for the Vecchio Library, which Fina had been cautious, but eventually grateful, for him to assume. It allowed her greater freedom to explore how the library could be made more useful and which institutions were discreet and reputable enough to receive pieces on loan. Slowly, she was revealing the library's riches to the world.

"Any decisions yet?" Beatrice asked.

Fina shook her head. "We have time. And Enzo is still young."

She knew the struggles both of them faced in their relationship. Knew that no one could make those decisions for them. She did know a quiet agreement had taken place between her husband and Zeno that if Fina did choose to become a vampire, Giovanni would act as her sire, as Zeno could not.

Beatrice had a feeling that the love the two shared would only grow with time. And when her son was old enough, Fina would choose to give up the day for her lover. But life was unexpected, and no one could make that decision except Fina.

"It's good to have friends," Beatrice said. "Especially those who know what you're going through. Don't hesitate to call. Or even—don't tell Zeno—e-mail me if you have a question."

Fina laughed and assured Beatrice she would. Then she took a glass of Antonia's wine out to her lover, who met her with an ardent kiss and a teasing smile. A vampire, yes. But also a man thoroughly in love.

Giovanni brushed a kiss on her shoulder. "Merry Christmas, Tesoro."

"Still no presents, Gio," she said with a sigh. "Not a single present. Ben's going to back me up on this one."

He chuckled and pulled her to her feet. "Come with me."

"What? Why? I was helping Angela cook. Kind of." She allowed him to lead her up the stairs as Angela's laughter followed them.

He led them to their suite of rooms, which had been redecorated after the nightmare of Beatrice's first visit to Rome when Livia still ruled. Now it was filled with rich reds and blues, colors that were vivid even at night. Art hung all over the walls and—because it was their room—books were stacked everywhere. It wasn't the neatest place, but she loved it.

"Okay, what is it?" she asked.

"Come here." Giovanni put his hands over her eyes and guided her across the room. "I did get you a present, though it's also a present for me. And, being very unoriginal, I got the same present for Zeno and Fina."

"Wow, so I was thinking lingerie, but now I'm really hoping that's not what it is, because that would be weird."

"Agreed." He pulled away his hands. "Merry Christmas."

It wasn't lingerie. But it was perfect. A page from Rafael's journal had been reproduced on vellum, looking so much like the original that she had to check the edges of the drawing. Floating over a mat of wine-red linen, the page was a drawing of Antonia looking over her shoulder, her dark curls tumbling down and mingling with the grape vines drawn on the hillside. She smiled, and the look the artist had captured in her eyes perfectly matched the contentment that Beatrice had seen earlier in Fina.

"I thought they'd like a copy, as well. To remember last Christmas. He really was an extraordinary artist, wasn't he?"

"It's perfect," she whispered, turning in his arms. "It's perfect, Gio."

"'She is all that is light and beauty in my life,'" Giovanni recited Rafael's words from his letter. "'My soul is but a mirror of her own. My heart, her twin in devotion. Surely God cannot condemn us. Surely the world must be kind. I will come for her, though oceans separate us…For what is an ocean against eternity?'"

"I love you."

"Merry Christmas."

THE END

Disclaimer

From the desk of Elizabeth Hunter

On behalf of all actual librarians, archivists, and other information technology professionals, I'd like to make it clear that real academic and historical research rarely, if ever, proceeds this quickly. Most of it takes months or years, but I didn't really have that much time in a Christmas novella. I just want to make it clear that *this is fiction.* (Then again, vampires who control the elements don't actually exist either, so you've probably guessed that I've taken a few liberties with the truth.)

Merry Christmas, everyone. And may this holiday season, let nothing be misshelved.

Read the books that launched a fictional universe:

THE ELEMENTAL MYSTERIES

A Hidden Fire
This Same Earth
The Force of Wind
A Fall of Water

The Elemental Mysteries, where history and the paranormal collide, and where no secret stays hidden forever. Join five hundred-year-old rare book dealer, Giovanni Vecchio, and librarian, Beatrice De Novo, as they travel the world in search of the mystery that brought them together, the same mystery that could tear everything they love apart.

"Elemental Mysteries turned into one of the best paranormal series I've read this year. It's sharp, elegant, clever, evenly paced without dragging its feet and at the same time emotionally intense."
—NOCTURNAL BOOK REVIEWS

"An enticing and addictive epic."
—Douglas C. Meeks, WICKED SCRIBES

"A tantalyzing paranormal romance, full of mystery and intrigue. One of the best books I've read in a long time. Sign me up for book two!"—Nichole Chase, NYT bestselling author of The Dark Betrayal Trilogy

ALSO BY GRACE DRAVEN

Master of Crows
Entreat Me
The Lightning God's Wife
Radiance

ALSO BY ELIZABETH HUNTER

The Elemental Mysteries Series
A Hidden Fire
This Same Earth
The Force of Wind
A Fall of Water
Lost Letters and Christmas Lights
(*novella,* All the Stars Look Down)

The Elemental World Series
Building From Ashes
Waterlocked (novella)
Blood and Sand
The Bronze Blade (novella)
Shadows and Gold:
An Elemental Legacy novella
(December 2014)

The Cambio Springs Series
Long Ride Home (short story)
Shifting Dreams
Five Mornings (short story)
Desert Bound (October 2014)

The Irin Chronicles
The Scribe
The Singer
The Secret (Winter 2015)

Contemporary Romance
The Genius and the Muse

About the Authors

Looking for any excuse to delay in doing the laundry, GRACE DRAVEN turned to the much more entertaining task of telling stories about fantasy worlds, magic, antiheroes, and the women who love them. She currently lives in Texas with her husband, kids, and a big doofus dog. Laundry has now been assigned to the kids.

More about Grace and her books can be found here:

http://GraceDraven.com

ELIZABETH HUNTER is a contemporary fantasy, paranormal romance, and contemporary romance writer. She is a graduate of the University of Houston Honors College and a former English teacher. She once substitute taught a kindergarten class, but decided that middle school was far less frightening. Thankfully, people now pay her to write books and eighth-graders everywhere rejoice.

She currently lives in Central California with her son, two dogs, many plants, and a sadly dwindling fish tank. She is the author of the *Elemental Mysteries* and *Elemental World* series, the *Cambio Springs* series, the *Irin Chronicles*, and other works of fiction.

http://ElizabethHunterWrites.com

Made in the USA
Middletown, DE
18 November 2017